GENTLEMEN

GENTL

EMEN

MICHAEL NORTHROP

SCHOLASTIC PRESS
NEW YORK

7-09

1699

Library of Congress Cataloging-in-Publication Data
Northrop, Michael.
Gentlemen / Michael Northrop. — 1st ed.
p. cm.
Summary: When three teenaged boys suspect that their English teacher is responsible
for their friend's disappearance, they must navigate a maze of assorted clues, fraying
friendships, violence, and Dostoevsky's *Crime and Punishment* before learning the truth.
ISBN-13: 978-0-545-09749-9
ISBN-10: 0-545-09749-5
[1. Guilt — Fiction.   2. Missing persons — Fiction.   3. Teachers — Fiction.
4. Crime — Fiction.   5. Friendship — Fiction.   6. High schools — Fiction.
7. Schools — Fiction.]   I. Title.
PZ7.N8185Ge   2009
[Fic] — dc22   2008038971

10 9 8 7 6 5 4 3 2 1   09 10 11 12 13

Printed in the United States of America   23

First edition, April 2009

The quotations from Fyodor Dostoevsky's *Crime and Punishment* are from the 2003
Bantam Classic reissue, translated by Constance Garnett, published by Bantam Dell, a
division of Random House, Inc.

The display type was set in Copperplate Gothic.
The text type was set in Adobe Garamond.

Book design by Phil Falco

TO THE LOCALS,
        THE RAGGIES,
AND THE REST

1

It started out as just another Tuesday at the Tits: first period, Practical Mathematics, nothing special. Name aside, there was nothing all that practical about the class. It was just math, simple math, math for dummies. They didn't figure we were up to geometry or that kind of stuff, and mostly they were right, so they just sat us down and drilled us with the basics.

It was a sunny spring day outside, but we were stuck at our desks doing square roots. When I say we, I mean me, Tommy, Mixer, Bones, and the rest of 10R. Tattawa is a small high school. We call it the Ta-Ta's or the Tits — another long day at the Tits, we'd say. There are four levels of classes at the Tits and R is the last one. 10R is tenth grade, remedial. It's not too hard to grasp. The other students joked like the *R* was for *Retard*, but they didn't joke to the four of us. We'd kill them. And we didn't think twice about telling them what *A* stood for.

I started out in 9A, in case you're wondering, one down from honors. I'd done OK on the test they made us all take back at the end of eighth grade. Better than OK, but the classes didn't work out. They said I wasn't "applying myself," and that's fair enough. Then I threw Oscar Tully a serious beating for saying something he shouldn't've, and that was that, down to general in the middle of the third marking period. I had no idea what was going on in G, and I didn't really feel like trying to figure it out. Sophomore year started and I found myself in 10R.

Fine with me, that's where someone like me belongs — someone of my "pedigree," if you read me. This should clue you in: My first name is spelled wrong. It's Micheal instead of Michael. Mom or Dad, one of them dropped the ball on that one, probably Dad, in the hospital or wherever it is you fill out that paperwork. Not that it matters; everyone calls me Mike. Still, it's a bad way to start things out. My grade school diploma reads: "This diploma hereby signifies that MICHEAL BENTON has blah blah blah." The first time I looked at it, I half expected it to have red ink on it, like, −2, *sp*. Like that should have been a proud moment, right? But it just had no chance.

I like 10R all right: I'm smart here, and it's where my friends are. But don't think it's like some fun club. There aren't that many of us in R, and we see a lot of each other.

We're just as likely to get under each other's skin as not. And we're not all alike. It's not like you see on TV, kids pushed through high school and still can't read.

Three small elementary schools feed into the Tits: Soudley, Little River, and North Cambria. Small towns, small classes, all mother-henned by the teachers . . . The only ones who can't read after nine years of that are the special ed kids, and they get shipped off to their own little center up on Route 7. I think they like canoe and paint all day. I heard that once.

Don't get me wrong, we've got some real morons, kids who just don't get it. Then there's us. They call us hard cases, and we are. They say we don't try, and we don't. We're not going to be engineers or accountants or anything like that. We're going to put in our time, because you need that diploma now, even to work down at the garage. Then that's pretty much what we're going to do, go work down at the garage or something like that, overcharge the same dipsticks we went to school with when they bring in their Volkswagens. In the meantime, we're stuck behind these little desks.

Me, I think I'd like to work outside: gardener, landscaper, that kind of thing. I'd get a truck and plow snow in the winter. Mixer's dad does that. Seems like a sweet deal. We could do this stuff if we wanted, Tommy, Mixer, Bones, and me. Well, maybe not Bones so much, if I'm being honest.

Anyway, like I said, Tuesday morning and we were doing square roots. Mr. Dantley was going up and down the rows. He'd give you a number and you were supposed to tell him the square root: no calculators, just paper and pencil, if you wanted. Sometimes he'd say something like 529 or whatever, and whoever got that one would be like, "I don't know" or "It doesn't have one." Mostly, they were easier.

When my turn came, Dantley looked at me and kept looking. He didn't look down at his list the way he did with the others. He looked at me for a long second. Now, people will do that, because of the way my eye is, but he'd seen that plenty of times before, so that wasn't it. He just eyeballed me and said, "One hundred twenty-one."

And I was like, Fine, if you want to play it that way, and I looked straight at him, didn't even look down at my notebook, and said, "Eleven."

It was on the frickin' times tables. I knew that in like fourth grade. He knew I did. He wasn't trying to stump me. I don't know what he was trying to do. These teachers were always trying to get inside my head. They always said it was for my own good, and I was always like, Whatever, I just don't want anybody in there, all right? Anyway, he gave me this little smirk, like he'd proved something, even though I was the one who got it right.

Tommy was next, and Dantley might've been working some angle with me, but he had real issues with Tommy. Those two were one hundred percent under each other's skin. Now, it's true that most teachers didn't like Tommy. He was "disruptive" even by 10R standards. He was loud, fidgety, always up to something. Anyway, Dantley got to Tommy and he said, "Nine." He looked down at his list, but you just knew he didn't read it off there. It was a special order, just for Tommy.

It was cold, and just cold on so many levels. First off, it was way too easy. Forget times tables, a five-year-old could've gotten that one. It was insulting, and he meant it to be. Secondly, Tommy couldn't say *three*. It was something about the *th* and the *r* back to back. I'd heard him try a few times. It came out too quick, too loud, and just sort of wrong.

Max went to elementary school with him in North Cambria and said that there used to be a lot more things Tommy couldn't say; *thr*-words were just the last holdouts. Anyway, it was the damndest thing. There were a few words like that, like *thrifty* or *thrust* or whatever, but, I mean, you don't have to say *thrifty* if you don't want to — kind of have to go out of your way to say it — but *three*, well, that'll come up from time to time. Generally speaking, that'd be in math class.

If we were solving problems out of the book, he would count ahead and see which one he was going to get. I'd seen him do it tons of times. Then he'd work the problem quick. Like I said, we weren't dumb, and he could solve those things easy with that kind of motivation. Anyway, if there wasn't a three in the answer, no sweat, he'd just chill until it was his turn. Then, like I said, he'd already have the thing solved. But if there was a three, well, his hand would go up for the bathroom or to get something from his locker. Like he'd pocket his calculator and say he forgot it. Worst-case scenario, he'd just get it wrong.

But now, I mean, what could he do? This question was too easy to get wrong and it was too late to head to the john. I sort of half turned around to see what he would do, or to see him try to squeeze out another one of those spastic threes of his. And do you know what he did? He flipped his frickin' desk over! Seriously, no kidding, he put his palms under the front edge and then threw it up in the air.

His head jerked back with his shaggy hair flying. His books, his notebook, his calculator, and all that stuff went flying. The desk crashed down, hit the back legs of my chair, and kind of scooted me forward a few inches. I couldn't believe it, none of us could. Dantley definitely couldn't. He just stood there for a moment, his mouth hanging open like a goldfish's.

I expected Tommy to be all red-faced and mad, but when I looked at his face, he looked just as surprised as the rest of us, like someone else had thrown the desk. I figured he'd just lost it or panicked or whatever. When I thought about it a little more, I switched my guess and figured it was because Natalie was in the class. Tommy had it bad for her. He always said so anyway, and then when he was around her he was totally tongue-tied, like he had no idea what to say to a girl, like he'd never had it bad for one before. It was completely uncool, so I figured he meant it.

The class was sort of split as to who was the hottest chick. The other contender was Nicole. She had a big rack for a sophomore, which can happen when it's your second or third year as one. Natalie wasn't packing much up top, but she had a nice face and long legs and I figured that's what Tommy went for. He was always a little less boob-obsessed than the rest of us. He didn't talk about them as much, he didn't draw them in his notebook like Bones did, and I never remember him pointing out a good pair coming down the hallway.

As for Natalie, she was supposed to be seeing this guy who didn't go to the school, probably didn't go to any school. People said they'd seen him pick her up in a sweet sports car out by the edge of the student parking lot, but no one could agree what kind of car it was, much less anything about the guy.

Anyway, Tommy always said he had it bad for her, and I figured he probably didn't want to embarrass himself in front of her. It's kind of funny that he thought flipping a desk was less embarrassing than screwing up the word *three*, but maybe he thought it would seem hard-core or something. But he was seriously out of luck now.

Dantley pulled it together and started yelling. Teachers don't like to be challenged physically. He knew we could tear him apart if we wanted to, so he had to make a show of being in charge, and that's what he did. He didn't hit Tommy or anything, but he yelled until the spit was coming out. Faces began appearing at the little window on the door. Faces of teachers, kids with hall passes, wondering what all the shouting was about.

Tommy just took it, just sat there in his chair with no desk. Pretty much, anyway. He gave Dantley some looks, but he kept his mouth closed. He was in enough trouble already, more than he probably meant for. Dantley got it out of his system, told Tommy to pick up his desk and his stuff, and sent him to Trever, the assistant principal. Trever was the hatchet man. He and Principal Throckmarten had a pretty well-polished good cop/bad cop thing going. I'm sure they'd been doing it since long before we arrived. Trever was a big black dude, which you didn't see much of around here, and I think that intimidated some of the kids.

I didn't say anything to Tommy when he walked by me; I just sort of let out some air, like, *phhhhhh!* as if to say, Man, you are one crazy dude, but I guess he could have taken it as, Man, you've got some big ones. I like to think he did.

We were still talking about it after class. When Mixer and I got to second period, I told Mr. Grayson, "Tommy will be a little late. He's with Trever."

"What's his offense this time?" Grayson asked.

I knew he'd ask that. It was kind of his standard line in that situation. I shrugged, like it was no big deal, then I said, "He threw a desk."

. Grayson raised his eyebrows and made a little whistle sound, which most of us thought was pretty funny. Grayson was the coolest teacher we had, which was kind of like being the best-smelling fart but still. He lights things on fire, drops them in acid, and once he took us outside to watch him set off a model rocket. I guess he has an advantage over the other teachers with things like that, because he teaches science, but he's also kind of more on our frequency.

Last winter, when I was in A, he held up a sparrow that'd hit the little glass walkway between the library and the main building. He held it up by its feet, or whatever they're called — I don't know if sparrows have talons, exactly — and it was frozen stiff. It was like a birdcicle. I mean, he must've seen it and gone out into the snow to pick it up, just so he could hold it up in front of the class. It's not the kind of thing most teachers would've done.

So anyway, we're basically cool with Grayson. We call him Mr. G, and that's the same thing we called him in class and when he wasn't around. Most of the teachers, we didn't address at all in class and called them like Mr. Doucheley when they weren't around. The class was about amoebas, and we were looking at diagrams on the overhead of little organisms with like hairs to move around with, just microscopic little goo-bags, basically. And the whole time we're expecting Tommy to come back, and the whole time he doesn't.

The bell went off and still no Tommy, so we knew he was really in deep. I had to go back to my locker to get my books for the next two classes. I don't like to carry too many books at once, and they don't let us carry backpacks around school since Wakeland got shot up last year, so it's replace math and science with Spanish and English. English was only one little paperback book, because we'd taken the test on the last one the day before, so I could've taken another book or two, but I didn't need to, because I had lunch and then gym after that. But I was really dragging, because Spanish was the worst and the English teacher was a total jackass. If I could, I would've skipped straight to lunch. It was sloppy joes, and even the school version of those wasn't that bad.

So anyway, I was swapping out my books and Mixer came over from his locker, which is pretty much straight across the hallway from mine.

"Wanna see something?" he said, and I was like, "Sure."

Now, when most people ask you if you want to see something, you just stand there and say, What is it? But with Mixer, you've got to go through this whole production. I knew the drill, so I opened my locker up a little more, like ninety degrees, and then stood in front of it. That blocked off people on the door side and out in front of it. Then Mixer closed in and blocked off the other side, and we had like a nice little nook to look at whatever it was without anyone else seeing.

All this effort put a lot of pressure on Mixer to have something cool, and he usually did. Mixer was liable to show up with anything at any time, because Mixer stole things. So now he took out this little folding knife from his pocket. It was small but totally sweet. He pulled the blade out and I could hear the little pop when it locked into place. All the good knives locked like that. The blade was maybe two inches long, maybe not even, but you could see it was super sharp. The handle wasn't wood, like my crappy jackknife, but some kind of knobbly orange plastic. It looked like official emergency gear or something.

"And you know the best thing?" he said. "I can hide this bad boy anywhere!"

"Nice," I said. "Sweet."

"Yeah," he said. "Thanks."

I waited till he'd folded it and put it away before closing the locker, because I'd made that mistake before. I didn't bother to ask where he got it or if he'd gotten me one. Mixer didn't see himself as Wal-Mart or Robin Hood or anything like that. He just saw himself as a guy who liked cool things. Like, if you were thinking that's an awful nice watch for a dirtbag sophomore to be wearing, you'd be right. He got it at the town lake when some yuppie douche bag took it off to go for a swim. Opportunities like that were the main reason Mixer went to the lake, and why yuppie douche bags should really consider buying waterproof watches.

Anyway, we were thinking we might see Tommy at his locker, since it was just a few down from mine, but he wasn't there. Mixer looked over, shrugged, and went back to his side of the hall. I wouldn't see Tommy in Spanish, either, because he'd opted for some other "elective," which couldn't've been any worse and was probably better, but I figured I'd catch up to him in English.

I'm Miguelito in Spanish — "little Michael" — because

there's a junior in the class named Michael. It sucks to be called Miguelito. I should be Migeul, anyway, then my name could be misspelled in two languages. Also, I was just not good at Spanish, so Miguelito basically translated to "wrong answer" as far as the rest of the class was concerned. I kind of had a problem with thinking the first thing that popped into my mind was the right answer. I did that in all my classes, but especially in Spanish, where the first thing I thought was often the only thing I knew. And classes like Spanish weren't broken up into levels, so it was pretty much everyone for themselves. My fault for taking it, but I thought it would be cool. I guess I was thinking like Zorro or something: El Bandito Mucho. I was wrong.

Spanish dragged on, like it always does. When I got to English, there was this weird setup in the front of the room, and Mr. Haberman had this twisted look on his face. He was standing in front of a blue plastic barrel and watching us file in, and I just was not in the mood for whatever it was he was up to.

The barrel was off to the side of Haberman's big hardwood desk. The barrel looked sort of familiar, but I couldn't place it and wasn't sure anyway. As for the desk, he'd told us more than once that it was his own, and you could see from two miles out that it wasn't like the flimsy fake-wood desks the other teachers parked behind. He'd also told us more than once that he didn't need this job, meaning he was rich or something, and that he could walk away anytime. Every time he said that, every single one of us was thinking, Well, go ahead. Bones'd carved *Mr. Homoman* into the wood on the front of the desk, along with a picture of this bent-over little dude. I don't know if Haberman ever noticed.

Tommy's desk was empty, and I saw Mixer come in with Bones and we started talking, fast and low, like, No way, did they send him home? Do you think they suspended him, just like that, on the spot? We were all asking the same questions, and none of us had any answers, and people were coming up to us to ask if we'd heard anything, because we knew him best, but like I said, we hadn't heard squat.

It was pretty loud, and then Haberman banged something against the side of the barrel, and it made this loud *buh-DUMP! buh-DUMP!* sound and that was his way of telling us to sit down, shut up, and see what's up with the barrel. Once it was more or less quiet, he cleared his throat. He was a seriously heavy smoker. You'd see him out front, sucking down one cigarette after another between classes. I'd never seen anyone smoke that fast. He worked the thing like it was a straw in an extra-thick milk shake, and figure he'd started smoking at fifteen or sixteen, he'd probably been sucking 'em down for thirty or forty years. So anyway, whenever he cleared his throat, it sounded like there was furniture moving around in there. Kind of made you cringe. Then, like always, he said, "Good morning, class."

He said morning even though it was one class to go before lunch, but the clock said it wasn't noon yet, and so he said good morning to us before class. It was this little tug-of-war he did with us. We wanted the day to be getting on and getting over, and he wanted to hold us right where we were. In Haberman's world, it was always morning, it was always some crappy Tuesday morning, and that was just the way he liked it. He would've liked us to respond with Good morning, Mr. Haberman, and I'm sure some classes did, but we weren't one of them. Some of us nodded at him but that was about it.

"All right, then," he continued. His voice was sort of tweety and gravelly at the same time, like a bird caught in a cement mixer. That was the cigarettes again. He must've had a girl's voice once. Tommy, Bones, Mixer, and me, we all smoked, but not like that. We couldn't score that many cigarettes, first off.

"This book we're about to start is a particular favorite of mine," said Haberman, "and as you can see, I will be going to some unusual lengths to attempt to teach it to you. I have a little teaching aid here to start with."

I looked around, expecting someone to stand up. I thought a teaching aid was a person, but I guess I was wrong. Maybe that's a teacher's aid.

"What do you suppose this is?" he continued. He gestured toward the blue plastic barrel with his right hand, sort of sweeping toward it so that you could see the palm of his hand, like this was a game show and the barrel was the prize. It was the kind you'd use to catch rainwater or hold the sort of heavy-duty junk that'd poke through garbage bags. It still looked kind of familiar. There was a little notch taken out of the lip of the thing, and I felt like I knew it'd be there, which would've meant I'd seen it before. But I couldn't think where that might've been. Maybe I'd just noticed that when I walked in.

"A barrel," said Reedy from the back of the room. We didn't raise our hands in here, because sometimes Haberman would leave you hanging for a while, hand in the air, dick in the wind, before calling on you. I guess he was waiting to see if anyone else would raise their hand, but why would you do that if someone else was already going to answer? What are we, going to fight over it?

"That's right," said Haberman. "It's a barrel. Can we all agree to that?"

It seemed like maybe he was insulting us. Of course it was a barrel. No one answered him exactly, but there were enough of those small noises that basically meant, Yeah, OK, that he moved on.

"And what do you suppose is in it?"

He held up both of his hands and shrugged his shoulders, and we could see that he had a piece of wood in his left hand. It was like one of those little clubs you used to brain fish once you hauled them onto the dock. That would've been what he hit the barrel with before.

I looked from the club to the open top of the barrel. You could see some blanket, dark wool and scratchy-looking.

"A blanket," I said. I don't know why I spoke up. I guess I

felt like someone had to or he'd just keep at it. Also, I didn't want to just sit there and be insulted. I'd get into it with him, if that's what he was angling for.

"An awfully big blanket, wouldn't you say?"

"What?" I said.

"An awfully big blanket. It must be quite large to fill up this whole barrel. More like a tent, I should think."

"It's not a tent."

"Well, an awfully, awfully big blanket, then . . ."

"Something wrapped in a blanket . . . *then*," I said.

"Ah, yes, I believe you are onto something, Mr. Benton. In fact, I will concede the point. It is, in fact, something wrapped in a blanket."

"What?" I asked, because he was still playing with us, and I'd just as soon get this over with.

"Ah, what, indeed," said Haberman. "Now we are approaching the heart of the matter."

He paused now and scanned the room. If he'd made a point, I'd missed it, but he stood there to let it sink in, anyway.

"I'll tell you what I'm going to do," he said. "I'm going to let each of you try to figure that out. What, oh what, is contained within this barrel, wrapped, as Mr. Benton informs us, within this blanket? It could be anything, so I'm going to let each of you investigate, albeit, in a very limited manner."

We sat back in our chairs, slouching, trying our best to look like we couldn't care less, but I'll give it to Haberman, we were all kind of wondering now.

"You each get," he said, taking a half step back and smacking the side of the barrel with the fish club — *buh-DUMP!* — "one whack."

Reedy whispered something about the whole class whacking off and the back of the room cracked up a little. Haberman ignored it, just stood up there behind the barrel, a fish club curled inside his fingers with their yellowed nails and a weird smile twisting on his lips.

"Let's begin at the beginning, shall we?" he said, extending his right hand toward Lara, first seat, first row, and gesturing for her to come over.

Lara was one of those girls, not exactly fat but definitely pushing the envelope, who wouldn't be allowed to be a cheerleader at a less crappy high school. But she was one at ours, and even though it wasn't a game day, wasn't even football season, she was dressed like it: a short blue skirt showing plenty of her thighs and sneakers with no socks. Being a cheerleader wasn't a big deal here, like it was some places, just like being on our football team didn't put a crown on your head. The preppy types, chicks included, played soccer in the fall, and the hard kids didn't do sports, so that left the kids in the middle for football and cheerleading.

Lara wasn't exactly sure what to do. She just got up and stood in front of Haberman, like she was reporting for duty, and he took her hand and put the little wooden club in it. She tapped the barrel with it, super light, like it was made of glass. The wood just sort of plinked off the plastic. I was thinking, How the hell is she supposed to get a read on what's in there from that? And sure enough, she had no idea.

"What do you think is in the barrel, Ms. Bialis?" Haberman asked. He called everyone by their last name. Hers sounded like a prescription drug.

Then it was like she realized her mistake, and she went to hit the thing again, harder, but Haberman grabbed the club from her on the backswing and said, "One per customer, Ms. Bialis."

"Well, I don't know," she said with a shrug. "Bunch of sand, I guess."

So Haberman was all like, "A bunch of sand!" Super dramatic, like a game show host again. I watched a lot of game shows, because my mom liked them. Then Haberman put the club down on top of the blanket in the barrel. The club stayed there, sort of sunk in, so that told me something. The blanket was lying flat along the top, and it was not stuffed full. He turned around, picked up a broken stick of chalk, and wrote *SAND* on the board. Then he turned back around and said, "Mr. Biron," meaning Max, first row, second seat back.

Max gave the thing a good whack and said, "A big watermelon."

"Excellent," Haberman said and wrote *WATERMELON* on the board.

It went on like that for a bit, Haberman writing down each guess, and then it was my turn. As I walked up to the front of the room I was thinking that this was totally unlike Haberman. I mean, this was English class; the only props we ever had in here were books. I was thinking this was something that Mr. G would do, and I was wondering if Haberman knew we liked Mr. G and hated him and was trying to like steal some of his thunder. I took the club from him and weighed it in my palm, you could feel the sweat and grease on it from the other hands, but it was a good, solid club.

I glanced over at the guesses so far. A lot of them were types of plants: watermelon, tree stump, things like that. Bridgit guessed clay, which wasn't a plant but sort of had that feel to it. I was thinking something along those lines, and I hauled off and really slammed the side of the barrel. I hit a knuckle on the plastic and the club stung my palm, but I stood there real still, trying to read the vibrations.

There was definitely something solid in there, and then a little liquid give at the center. Watermelon was a good guess, but I didn't want to copy Max. Plus, whatever was in there was big. It was tough to get an exact read, but too big to be a watermelon, except maybe at the farm exhibits at the Big E. What did it feel like? And then it came to me.

"Meat," I said. "Some kind of meat."

A few of the girls were like, Ewww, and then there was laughter in the back of the room. I figured that Reedy'd probably said something about me beating my meat, so I gave him a look. He looked down quick, but I could see he was smiling, so I knew I was right.

"Meat," said Haberman, as if he'd never heard the word before and he was mulling it over. "Very interesting."

He wrote it on the board and I sat down. This went on for a while, burning up like half the class. It was sort of interesting at first, but by the time it'd snaked around to the last desk, we pretty much got the point. Finally, there were fourteen guesses on the board, one for each student, and Haberman was ready to settle in on a nice boring lecture. Sometimes he just pulled what he said out of his ass, but you could tell that he'd put some thought into what came next. It sounded planned out, *rehearsed* is the word.

"What do we have here?" he said, putting the little club into a drawer in his desk and turning back to look at the board. He looked at it like he'd just come across it, like he wasn't the one who just wrote all of those words and there wasn't still chalk dust on his fingertips. He should've known by then that we didn't respond to open questions like that, and one little stunt with a barrel wasn't going to change that. He remembered, I guess, and without turning around, he said, "Mr. Benton? What do we have here?"

I wasn't sure why he was singling me out, so I kept it simple. "A list."

"That's right, Mr. Benton. We have a list. A list of what?"

"A list of words."

"Yes. It is that, but what else is it?"

He turned around, but he wasn't looking at me. He was

looking around the room. I guess he was looking for someone who might answer his question, but there were no takers.

"These," he said, waving behind him, "they are words, but what else are they?"

There was still no response — the kind of no response where you could imagine hearing crickets.

"This," he said, stabbing his finger into the *W* in *watermelon*, "what is this?"

I thought he was going to call on me again, but he didn't.

"Mr. Reed, you seem to have a lot to say today" — Haberman heard every whisper, he just didn't react to most of them — "so what is this?"

"Uh, watermelon," Reedy said in a fake-dumb way designed to get laughs, but he only got a few little snorts.

"Is it? Is it, really? Do you like watermelon, Mr. Reed?"

"Yeah, it's OK."

"Well, then, would you like a slice? Why don't you come up here and take a slice of delicious watermelon?"

He circled the word in chalk as he said it, so we knew he was talking about what was on the board and not what was in the barrel. Reedy thought it was a joke or something and didn't say anything, but after a while you could tell that Haberman was waiting for him to respond.

"I can't," Reedy said.

"Why not? You say it's watermelon." He circled it again. "Come up here and have some nice watermelon."

And now Haberman was sort of glaring at Reedy, like he was angry at him for saying it was watermelon. Reedy looked over at the barrel. He'd guessed a jug of water.

"It's not a real watermelon," Reedy said, and you could see he was sort of uncomfortable now. The way Haberman did that, switched from smiling and joking to angry, so that you knew he wasn't really joking in the first place, it could creep you out if you were on the receiving end of it.

"What is it then?"

"It's a word . . ."

"No!" said Haberman. It was almost a shout, and Reedy sat there squirming in his seat as Haberman went on a long coughing jag from the stuff he'd kicked up in his lungs. When he was done, he picked up like it hadn't happened.

"That is not wrong, Mr. Reed, it is merely redundant."

Reedy gave him a blank look.

"Mr. Benton has covered that, I believe. I asked what else it is. What else is it?"

Reedy just kept beaming that blank look, and Haberman broke out into a smile again. So now it's like he wasn't really mad. He was a strange dude. He looked at me, and I probably had half a smile on, because it's funny if this stuff isn't happening to you, and I knew what he was going to say, anyway.

"It is an idea."

He looked around after he said it like he expected us all to fall out of our chairs from the sheer amazingness of this. When we didn't he just went on.

"It is not a real watermelon. It is a guess, Mr. Biron's guess. Maybe there is a watermelon in the barrel, and maybe there isn't. In fact, I will tell you that there is not. If you were to come up here and attempt to lift this barrel, you would know that whatever it is that's in there, it is far too heavy to be a watermelon. So there is no actual watermelon, either in the barrel or on the board. So what does that leave us with?"

Haberman's pace was picking up, so we knew he was going to answer his own question without risking one of us getting it wrong.

"It leaves us with the idea of a watermelon. Mr. Biron hit the barrel. He thought about what he heard, what he felt, and it seemed to him like a watermelon. Is that fair to say?"

He looked at Max, who nodded and said, "Yeah."

"Perhaps you even pictured a watermelon, with that green, mottled rind, and that classic ovoid shape?"

Max didn't know what at least a few of those words meant, and I knew one and not the other, but he shrugged and said, "Sure."

"That is what we have here: a word signifying the idea of a watermelon. In fact, we have many words signifying many ideas. Not all of them can be right. Actually, little secret here, none of them are. Though one is close."

He didn't look at anyone in particular when he said this, so we didn't know who was close.

"But the ideas are still there. The sand that Ms. Bialis may have imagined running through her fingers, may have remembered from a trip to the Cape, it is up on this board. We have, let's see, fourteen ideas up on the board, and though none of them match the contents of this barrel, they are all, in their own way, just as real."

I was looking at the barrel and thinking, Christ, if that's the point he wanted to make, he could've used a Dixie Cup, a Dixie Cup with something wrapped in a napkin, and we could have flicked the side with our fingers. Haberman paused to cough up more lung butter, then continued.

"If I were to tell you what's in this barrel, not show, but just tell, would it be any more real? You would not be able to see it or touch it. It would exist only in your mind. Suppose, for example, I was lying?"

The smile crept back onto his face.

"And here are two more for you to ponder," he said, turning away.

Haberman picked up the chalk and wrote on the board. We couldn't see what he was writing, since he made a better bore than a window, but when he stepped back we could see two new words at the end of the list: *CRIME* and *PUNISHMENT.* We'd seen those words before, since that was the book he'd handed out the week before. It was on most of our desks, *Crime and Punishment*, by some Russian dude.

Haberman gave all his classes the same books. It was like a point of pride or whatever. He said, actually said to us, that he could teach Melville to a stone — hard to miss the point there, looking down at the new copy of *Moby-Dick* on your desk — and maybe he could, if he made the questions easy enough. The first question on our test had been "What kind of animal was Moby-Dick?" But that didn't mean he wouldn't put us through a lot of hot air along the way. We figured he gave the same little speeches to all his classes, too, about metaphors and allusions and shadows in caves.

We figured this latest book would just be more of the same. So now that he brought it up it was like he actually had a point with all of this barrel crap, and we were probably getting to it. Still, it felt like Tommy could walk in right now, lean over and say, What'd I miss? And I could say, Nothing much, and not be far off. He'd say, What's with the tub? And I'd just shrug. I looked over at the door but there was no one there.

"And what are these?" said Haberman, flicking the point of the chalk back and forth between the two new words. "Mr. Benton?"

And it was pretty clear he wanted me to say ideas, but I didn't exactly want to be his go-to guy, so I held up my copy of the book and said, "Homework."

I got a few laughs out of that line and Haberman frowned, but before he said anything, Lara was like, "Ideas!" She was truly happy to figure this one out, like a puppy finding a squeak toy.

"That's right!" he said, turning toward her.

She leaned forward, in case he asked her something else, but he just plowed ahead on his own.

"What is a crime? What is it really? It is the idea that someone has done something wrong. One person may consider something a crime, and another person might consider it something else. The characters in this book certainly cannot agree. Is a fight in the hallway a crime? It fits the definition of assault, but it is more likely to end in detention after school than in a courtroom. Why is that? A minor has some wine in church; is that underage drinking or religious expression?"

And this is why people hate people like him. He wasn't wrong, exactly, but he was full of crap, because there are laws. Obviously. They're written down and if you break them and you aren't careful, you go to jail or get your head kicked in by the cops, and just because it hadn't happened to him or anyone he knew didn't mean it wasn't real, that it was all an idea. I do something serious and my life is flushed down the pipes, and sure, I might do it anyway, but that's a chance I'm taking, and I still know the fact of the matter. But he just kept going, acting like he was on a roll.

"And what is punishment? Well, it comes after a crime, doesn't it, after a crime or at least a transgression of some sort? The ideas are linked. They are universal. *Tsumi to batsu*, that is crime and punishment in Japanese. I don't know why I remember that; I just do."

And I was thinking: I don't know why I don't care; I just don't.

"The concept, and it is eastern as well as western, is that the crime creates an imbalance, and the punishment restores that balance. It is yin and yang or action and reaction, but is it true? Isn't it all just an idea? Couldn't you look at it differently? The crime changes things — a house that was standing is now burned down — and the punishment changes things more — a man that was free is now in jail. Excuse me, a man *who* was free. Is that more in balance or more out of balance? A case could be made either way. Ideas can be linked to one another, and they can also be at odds with one another. To an extent, everyone must be their own judge, their own jury. Think about that as you read this book. How does it apply to Raskolnikov? What is his conception of crime? Does it change over the course of the book?"

I was thinking, How does it apply to who? I looked at the clock and it was a little more than ten minutes to go before lunch, and that ten minutes went pretty much the same way. Haberman did the talking, and now he was talking about this dude Raskolnikov. It made me think of *rascal*, a word my gramps used to use. A minute or so to go and a few people actually raised their hands. Again, it wasn't something that happened much in here. Haberman picked Max, and Max goes, "So what's in the barrel anyway?"

Haberman curled his mouth up into half a smile, spread his hands, and said, "Ultimately, it doesn't matter. Whatever you think is in there, well, then that is what's in there. In every way that matters, the contents are in your mind, not in the barrel."

Which is the same crap he'd been saying all class and not an answer. One more example of why we didn't raise our hands much.

When the bell finally went off, he gave us our homework, adding another twenty-five pages to the twenty-five none of us had read the night before. We figured we'd find a one-page wrap-up of the book on the Internet before the test. Bones found a pretty good site for those last time. I didn't need it for that one, because I'd seen the movie, but I figured I'd check it out for this one. I didn't think there was a movie of *Crime and Punishment*. I hadn't heard of one, anyway. Maybe there was an old one, but I didn't watch any of that black-and-white crap.

2

We grabbed our stuff quick. Haberman's class was a haul from the cafeteria, and you didn't want to be at the end of the line and have to stand there forever like a tool. We'd sort of formed up around my desk, you know, assembling Strike Force Delta, but just as we were heading out, Haberman was like, "You three, Benton, Bonouil, and Malloy, a moment, please."

That's me, Bones, and Mixer, and we gave each other a quick look. We hadn't done squat and had no idea what this was about. It turned out he wanted help getting the stupid barrel out to his car. That still didn't answer the question of why us, and as the others pushed past you could see they were looking at us and thinking the same thing. He shouldn't have been allowed to just jack our lunch like that, but if we walked out, we'd be the ones in trouble.

Haberman was either lucky or good, because if he'd asked

just me, I'd just as likely've said no thanks and taken my chances. If I end up in detention with Tommy, then I end up in detention with Tommy. I knew the way. If Tommy was suspended already, well, then I'd be a full step up the ladder from him. Mixer probably would've done the same thing. Bones might or might not've. He was on the brink of failing in here. English is a core class and no one wanted to do tenth again, especially Bones. He'd already failed a grade once. The first time we met him was his second try at fourth grade.

He was pretty different back then. He was still called Gerard, for one, and he wasn't so angry. I mean, he was ten, and there's only so angry a ten-year-old is going to be. He was just hyper and a year older than the rest of us. It wasn't the kind of thing you discussed, but everybody knew. We'd seen him around in the hallways and the cafeteria, so we knew he wasn't new to the school, and we knew he hadn't been in our class the year before, so it wasn't too hard to piece together that he'd been held back. He just came with fourth grade, like the furniture.

You could tell it wasn't something he wanted to talk about, but he loosened up some in the second half of the year. He'd made two friends by then, the same two friends he had now, and the teachers mostly hadn't bothered to change the tests from the year before. Even the pop quizzes were mostly the same. He'd been left back one year, but in a way, it's like the teachers are left back every year. Anyway, he started giving Mixer and me a heads-up on the quizzes and tests, the ones he remembered anyway. It was probably the first and only time in his life he qualified as smart. But that was when the other kids turned on him. I guess maybe they wanted him to share the test info a little more widely.

Toward the end of the year, they started in on him. They'd be like, "So long! Say hi to the next class. We'll write you when we get to fifth grade, let you know how it is." I think that's when the anger really started to creep into his system. And then every year after that, the teachers handing his tests back face-up, a big red D or F on top, having to sweat it out every June, whether or not he was going to move ahead with the rest of us.

Hell, it even kind of makes me angry, thinking about the little kid he was back in fourth grade. He used to jump off the top of the slide and yell "Spider-Man!" We'd all be laughing and he'd be smiling and his face'd be bright red from the attention.

But that smile was gone now, and it's like all that was left were the Ds and Fs. And it's kind of funny, too, because all those little bastards who made fun of him were right: That kid, the kid he was, never really did make it out of fourth grade. And two years into high school, I was starting to suspect that I was friends with someone who didn't really exist anymore. Just sometimes he'd make an appearance, the old Bones, smiling out at me about some dumb thing and I couldn't help but smile back. We had a history, you know, and isn't that what friendship is?

Anyway, like I said, Haberman asked all three of us, so any one of us bailing kind of screwed the others. Plus, with three of us, it seemed like it would be quick and easy to haul the barrel out to the parking lot. Throw in the facts that Haberman had a sweet car and English was on the first floor, and we were just like, All right, whatever.

But we were wrong, because it turned out that he was not kidding about the barrel being heavy. A watermelon, my ass. At first we tried to slide it along the floor, but that didn't work at all. The blue plastic dragged along the tile, sticking more than it slid. The floor was smooth enough, but there was some kind of grit on the bottom of the barrel. We started to tip it over to roll it, but Haberman said no way, so we had to lift it. It was tricky to grip, so it took two of us to get the thing off the ground. Then Bones found some space in the middle and became like the outboard engine. He did most of the pushing us forward, while Mixer and me did most of the lifting. Haberman didn't even pretend he was going to help. He was just like, "This way," but we knew where the teachers parked.

There was the usual mob scene between classes. Kids who had early lunch period coming back, eating snack packs of Oreos and picking their teeth. Kids who had late lunch heading that way. People talking at their lockers, some couples kissing, and here we come like the hired help. I hated that. I hated how it made me feel. I knew they were looking at me, and normally I might shoot them a look or shoulder into them when I walked by, but it's hard to look tough when you're squatting down and red in the face, so I just kept my eyes straight ahead and kept my feet shuffling along.

"This frickin' sucks," I said, loud enough for Haberman to hear, and of course, I didn't really say frickin'. He didn't say anything. What did he care? We were the ones breaking into a sweat. Mixer and Bones sort of grunted their agreement. They knew what I was talking about. I knew everyone around us was like, There go those losers. Get used to the heavy lifting, boys. They're no better than me, but that's not what they were thinking then, and I just wanted to pop someone in the mouth.

We finally reached the big double doors. Haberman opened the one on the right, and he was like, "After you, gentlemen."

He always called us gentlemen. Any group of guys in the hallway or rolling into class a little late got one of those. He called the girls ladies. I wondered what he called the principal, Your Majesty? Anyway, it was like, Yeah, screw you very much, and we were through the doors and out into the sunlight and open air.

"I've got to put 'er down for a sec," said Mixer, and that was fine with me. We dropped the barrel at the top of the wide stone steps that led down into the front parking lot. Just three steps, real short and wide, so they wouldn't be a problem getting down. I straightened up, and for a second it was actually kind of cool. Being outside on a nice day was one

thing, but being outside on a nice day when you were supposed to be in the god-awful gloomy hallways of the Tits was
another thing entirely. Pretty nice.

"All right, then," said Haberman, like he was our boss and
not our teacher. Totally ruined it. We leaned back down,
wedged our fingers between the heavy plastic and the hard
granite. We lifted with our legs and not our backs, like we
learned when we helped Tommy's dad move into his apartment in the city. Gary, who told us that, was Tommy's stepdad
now. It was kind of a bad scene, that move, but it was good
advice.

"Not for nothing," said Bones, "but what the hell's in this
thing?"

"Are you recanting your guess, then, Mr. Bonouil?" said
Haberman.

"Yep. I'm recanting all of those guesses, everybody's."

"Everyone was wrong? Not one of your classmates hit the
jackpot?"

"Nope," said Bones. He was grinding his teeth and spitting out his words between huffs and puffs. He wasn't looking
at Haberman, but he was talking right at him, if that makes
any sense. He was talking to Haberman like he was a freshman and not a teacher. It's not a real offense, not like shoving
him or something, but it was close to one, especially the way
Bones was going about it.

Bones was just not good at this, at provoking people, picking arguments. He had no volume control, and everything he

said just sounded like a threat. This was more Mixer's game, and as long as Bones had hung out with Mixer, he never could pick it up. Bones lacked the mental tools for it, I guess, and the patience.

Mixer was excellent at this kind of thing, at needling people without giving them any real good excuse to smack him. Since fourth or fifth grade, he'd been able to get the other guy to start it, roomful of witnesses, and then pound the poor kid into the ground "in self-defense." With teachers, he could just piss them off without giving them any good cause for punishing him. You couldn't do it all the time, otherwise people would catch on. Mixer knew that. He saved it for special occasions, and he was smart about it.

Bones was always the other guy, the one it was easy to get going. If you wanted a fight, it'd take all of about three words to get Bones to go. And early on, that happened a lot. Back in elementary school, when he was just this skinny, aggressive kid, he used to get into a lot of fights. But at some point, I guess around sixth grade, he just stopped following the rules.

Kid fights don't usually have clear winners. Sometimes, like if somebody slips or takes one clean on the nose, yeah, it'll be pretty obvious. More often, kids just grab and paw and swing wide at each other until they get it out of their system. Then they stop when the one who's getting the worst of it decides to quit while he can still pretend he won, or at least call it a draw. The way to quit is to sort of pull back and stall until the teachers get there. Everyone knew the deal, but

Bones got to the point where he wouldn't stop until he was pulled off. Sometimes it took three of us.

That's when people stopped wanting to fight him. That's how he got the nickname, too. You might think it's because he's skinny, skin and bones, but that's not it. It's because pulling him off a kid in a fight was like pulling a dog away from a bone. And it might seem like it'd be hard to be friends with someone like that, but that's only half the story, because it was cool, too. It's like rappers have pit bulls, you know? And when kids stopped wanting to mess with him, they stopped wanting to mess with us. There wasn't much of a difference back then. We were tight. If Bones saw someone giving me trouble, he'd give it right back to them.

Haberman didn't know any of this, of course. He thought he was talking to a student, but really, it was like he was poking a dog with a stick. He was a teacher and that'd probably always been enough to keep him safe, just the name, the word. But Bones didn't put a lot of value in words. He could understand being in the school, just that there are different rules in there and walls and doors to hold him in place, but we were out of the school now. Just a few yards out, but those must've seemed like some long yards to Bones. His voice, his body language, it'd all changed from the hallway to here. He was coiling up, giving all the warning signs that anyone who'd gone to school with us would've recognized. But Haberman had never seen them before.

"And why do you suppose your classmates all got it wrong?" he said.

"Well, A, because you said so, and B, because they didn't have to lift it."

We arrived at Haberman's car and dropped the barrel near the trunk.

"Yes, this is the one. You three seem to know that already, though. I guess I know who to ask if my tires mysteriously sprout holes."

Yeah, we knew his car. It was a sleek little MG sports car. Vintage, dark red, real nice. There weren't any other cars like that in the teachers' lot. There was one sweet BMW in the student lot, but that was new. This thing was like an antique, but it ran smooth. I'd heard the engine hum by a few times.

We served detention in a little room that was just thirty or forty yards from here, and in the nice weather, the windows were open. Everyone sort of wondered why such a wreck of a teacher had such a sweet car — he made more noise coughing than the car made starting — but I guess it was just that family money of his. If I had that kind of money, I'd buy a car like that, too. I was counting the months till I got my license. There weren't too many left, but it felt like they were just crawling by.

"Well, then, Mr. Bonouil," said Haberman, getting back to Bones's question. "You have had to lift it. Knowing what you know now, after all of your hard-earned insight, would you like to revise your guess?"

"I'd prefer you just tell me," said Bones. He stood up straight and he was three, maybe four inches taller than Haberman. He could pound him into dog meat, and out here in the parking lot, it seemed like that just might happen. But Haberman just kept ignoring the vibe, running right through the red lights.

"Oh, I don't think you'd believe me if I did."

Now they were looking right at each other, and I was thinking, Don't do it, because it just wasn't worth it. Yeah, that sucked, hauling that thing past half the school and everything, but it was over now, so I broke in.

"Yeah, well, you better believe that this thing won't fit into that trunk," I said.

"Hmmm?" said Haberman, looking down and sizing things up a bit. "You're quite right, Mr. Benton. Sometimes, you know, I think you're holding out on me."

I ignored that last comment and said, "We'll have to dump it out. It'll probably fit without the barrel."

It would fit if there was any give to it, because the shape was the problem. So once again, the topic swung around to what was in the barrel. Haberman took the keys out of his pocket and unlocked the trunk, which rose open on its own once he removed the key. Just a few things in there: another blanket, like the one in the barrel but folded flat, a jug of water, and a jack. I didn't see the tire iron, but it might've been in the shadows farther back.

"You could've filled this thing up with lead shot, just to make us carry it," said Bones. I could tell he was still angry, because we'd stopped lifting, but his face was still red.

Mixer had been quiet this whole time. That's sort of what kept me from being too worried about it. Mixer was good at reading people, when they were likely to lose it, where that line was. Like I said, it was almost a game to him, and he could read Bones as well as anyone. I sort of figured, if anything was really going to happen, Mixer'd speak up. And he was speaking up now.

"Hey, Bones," he said. "Got any plans this summer?"

That must've seemed like a weird comment to Haberman, like totally random and out of the blue. There's a phrase for things like that: non-something, non-sensical, maybe? Anyway, Mixer had a point. He was telling him, in so many words, you do anything out here, anything at all, and you fail English. You fail English, and you go to summer school. Bones looked at him for a second, the anger was still in his eyes, but then he got it. He let his head roll back and around, like someone had just taken the spine out of his neck. He shook out his shoulders a little. He was making a show of calming down, letting us know it took some real effort.

Like I said before, Bones was Humpty Dumpty sitting on the wall when it came to English. He always kind of struggled in school, even when he had normal teachers, so Haberman was a nightmare, with all his mind games. At this point,

Bones could practically taste that F, and F is the first letter in summer school at best or repeating at worst, and he'd had enough of that.

"You read me?" said Mixer.

Bones let his head drop back down. He looked over at Mixer and nodded.

"Yeah, well, we're going to have to dump 'er out, whatever it is," said Bones, his voice more or less back to normal.

"I would certainly appreciate that," Haberman said, looking from Bones to Mixer and back with a little grin on his face.

"Whatever," said Bones. He crouched down and Mixer and me did the same, wedging our fingers under the barrel again.

"Ready," said Bones, making a show of being in charge, just to get a little dignity back. We nodded and let him have some. Then we lifted. We stood up, shuffled a few steps forward, and sort of leaned in, resting the side of the barrel against the lip of the open trunk. Now we had to sort of readjust and squat down again to grip the barrel farther back, so we could tip it forward.

It hadn't gotten any lighter, that was for sure, and the sweat had already started creeping out again. I was going to have pit stains, which sucked. We got under there and tipped the thing forward, but whatever was inside was wedged in good and snug with the blanket. We sort of shook the barrel, but it wasn't really working.

"Little help here," I said, and Haberman leaned in there, grabbed the top of the blanket, and gave it a good tug. It almost pulled the barrel out of our hands, and I was sort of surprised that Haberman had that kind of strength. As I was thinking this, the contents of the barrel slipped out like one long turd. It made a sound like *THWUP* as the sides of the blanket slid free from the plastic. As it went, we sort of pulled the barrel up and away and all of a sudden the barrel was empty and light, and there was this sort of tube-shaped mass of blanket hanging out of the edge of the trunk.

It was two blankets, I could see now, bound together with gray duct tape. Whatever was in there was wrapped tight, but you could see there was some sprawl to it. It didn't want to be tube-shaped like that, and it was pushing out against the tape and blankets at a few points.

We put the barrel down on the asphalt, and when I stood up again, there was like a knob or something pushing out against the wool near my left hand. I reached out to touch it, but I kind of didn't want to for some reason, and that's proba-bly why I was too slow. Haberman pushed in front of me and shoved the whole thing forward and down, stuffing it into the trunk. As he was pushing, the shape started breaking down and more sort of knobs appeared, pressing out against the blanket. But then it was in there, sort of taking the shape of the trunk.

"Excuse me, gentlemen," he said.

We stepped back and, just like that, he slammed the trunk. Then he did that thing with his hands, rubbing his palms together a few quick times, like he was brushing some dust off them, and it was like, Show's over, so long, thanks for coming. Mixer, Bones, and me were just standing there looking at the shiny paint on top of the closed trunk.

"Well, then, I suppose I can return this myself," Haberman said, and I sort of jumped because, as dumb as it sounds, I'd half forgotten about him. "You have earned yourselves a hearty lunch, certainly," he said.

He reached into his pocket and pulled out his wallet. It was old enough that the leather was worn smooth. He pulled out three dollar bills and gave us each a buck. I got the old crappy bill, which figured. You got the idea that he really thought that this'd cover it, that this guy could be at the school for decades and not know how much lunch cost or what exactly a sloppy joe was. A buck each was way below market rate for that kind of lugging — what was this, 1952? — but we took it. If he'd paid in advance, he might've spared himself some of the grief with Bones. But then, I'm not even sure he noticed the grief with Bones.

"Don't forget to retrieve your books from my room before you go," he said.

He picked up the barrel by the top edges and then sort of tossed it up, so he could wrap his arms around the sides. Now it was in front of him like a giant plastic cup. He started carrying the empty barrel back toward the school for some reason. We watched him for a second and then looked back at the trunk. We could've asked him again what that was; I knew we were all thinking it. But it was pretty clear he wasn't going to tell us at that point, and now I was starting to think that I didn't necessarily want to know.

It was the way it moved under the blankets, the way it shifted around. It seemed to have, I don't know, joints or something. I mean furniture can have joints, like a lawn chair or whatever, but that was no frickin' lawn chair.

3

Roadkill. That's what we figured it was. The three of us hashed it out over cold sloppy joes during what was left of lunch period. It took a little compromise. Mixer was just listing heavy things at first, more or less at random, but I told him it was flesh and bone, some kind of animal. I sort of put my foot down, and once I did, Bones agreed. He thought it was cool. Mixer climbed aboard, and after that, roadkill was the one thing we could all agree on. When we were listing possibilities, Bones said "Tommy," but he said it as a joke and we took it that way.

"About the right size," he added, even though it wasn't a funny enough joke to need a follow-up.

We figured it was a fawn, maybe a doe, terminated by someone's bumper. Not Haberman's. Even a small deer would do some serious damage to that little waterbug of a car. Of course, we were mostly looking at the trunk and not the hood, but if that thing had hit something, we would've seen some sign of it. It would've had to've been that day or maybe the night before, I told them, fresh, the way things were still shifting around under those blankets.

It wouldn't've been too hard to find a dead deer. Someone creams one in their pickup and just pushes it off to the side of the road or doesn't even bother. It happened all the time. I was in the car when Joey, Mixer's older brother, hit one last year. A buck, but on the smallish side, it'd bolted out of the woods that run along Undermountain Road.

It came from the far side so that it had to cross the empty lane before getting to us. But at the speed it was going, a flat-out sprint, gallop, whatever, there was no way it was going to be able to stop. No way we were, either, the way Joey drives, but he slammed on the brakes, practically stood up on them. It looked like the thing might make it, might just clear us, but it didn't quite get there. Joey clipped him, just barely. It was the passenger-side headlight that clipped the buck's hindquarters. The headlight popped out of its socket, and the deer flipped up onto the bank and broke its neck, clean.

We pulled over and walked back and the thing had its eyes open, but it wasn't so much as twitching. It was dead as dead gets, with a little stream of blood coming out its ear. Joey was pretty pissed about the headlight and it was almost dark, so we turned around half a mile up the road and headed back. We looked at the spot when we drove past but the deer was already gone. Somebody'd tossed it in the back of their truck and taken it home, a bonus deer, off-season.

This time of year, deer were everywhere, idiot young ones in tow. You got used to seeing broken glass along the side of the road. That'd ruin someone's day and maybe their life, too, if the deer made it up the hood and through the windshield. There was a pretty good chance of that, too, since they call them windshields and not deershields. Someone died that way once or twice a year around here.

The thing I remember about hitting that deer, there was a book on the seat next to me, a kids' book. It was called *The Happy Man* or something like that. It was for Joey's girlfriend's little kid. Joey still looks a lot like Mixer, but he's like seven or eight years older.

Anyway, I remember the book sliding forward, and it seemed real slow and fluid, like a lazy wave slopping onto a dock. Then it slammed into the seat back and flapped down onto the floor, and suddenly everything was back to full speed. It was the last thing I saw before I face-planted into the back of the headrest on Joey's beat-up old Saab.

I got a bloody nose, but it's amazing none of us ended up in the hospital. Joey had his seat belt on, because this was just after he started seeing Amy Krukowski, Amy K, and her having a kid and all made him into more of a buckle-up kind of guy. He was preparing for some real adulthood, I guess, and sure enough, they've got a little house now.

Anyway, that's what we figured it was, a deer carcass,

wrapped up in plastic to keep any blood in, and a few blankets to keep it a mystery. We figured it was Haberman's version of Mr. G's frozen bird, and if we were right, that man needed some serious help. We already knew that, but this was a whole new level of nuts. And that's why he wouldn't tell anyone what it was. He could get into some real trouble for bringing that much dead animal into a public high school. It was a long way from cutting up frogs in science.

"I hate that guy," said Bones, when we were talking about whether Haberman could get fired for something like that.

"We know!" said Mixer, and they both laughed.

I laughed some, too, but it was just reflex. You know how sometimes you start laughing when the people around you do, just to cover yourself until you figure out what's so funny? Because it hadn't been funny in the parking lot, and I figured Bones wasn't really joking.

Anyway, that was lunch. I had last-period study hall, which was like gold if you were a senior, because you could leave early. But it wasn't gold if you were a sophomore, it was still made out of the same crap as everything else at this school. There were no tests and no one was talking at you in study hall, but it was pretty boring and especially bad last period, when you could almost feel what it would be like to be home already, on the couch with a snack in one hand and the remote in the other.

I signed myself into the library for this one, which you can do if you get there early enough. I had to go to the library because I had to use a computer. I don't have one at home. I had to use a computer because I had to check my e-mail, and I had to check my e-mail because I can be a tremendous jackass sometimes, just a dangling set of donkey balls. Usually when I am, there's a girl involved. It's like magic: Instant donkey balls, just add girl.

I shouldn't be telling you this part. It's embarrassing as hell. A little background: The girls in this school had shown pretty much no interest in yours truly since day one. The only tits I ever got here were in the nickname, you know? And sure enough, thinking about the girls I thought were hot and the ones I thought were OK and the ones just below that who I'd actually tried to talk to, I was getting a big fat zero on the interest meter. I mean, they'd hear me out, but as soon as I turned around, they'd run back to their friends and I'd hear them giggling and whispering a mile a minute, and I knew what they were saying: donkey balls.

So anyway, with those kind of playing conditions on my home field, I'd had to cast kind of a wider net. The best place for that around here was at the Soudley town lake. Girls from other towns go there, because it was bigger and nicer than the other lakes around here. We even got tourists. I'd biked down there just about every day the summer before, which was going on a full year ago now. It was a better scene for me, because I could walk around in my swim shorts and wear a baseball hat down real low over my eyes. My left eye is messed up, and that side of my face a bit, but my body is just normal, so walking around like that sort of played up the normal part of me and played down the messed-up part.

In all that time down there, I met two girls. They were both named Jenny: Jenny #1 and Jenny #2 is as much as you need to know. Now, two girls doesn't seem so bad — the problem is that I met them within a day of each other. I was down there four or five days a week for months, I only met two girls, and I couldn't even get that right. I swear to god, sometimes I think I'm cursed.

So I met Jenny #1 on August 1, real pretty day, semi-pretty girl. At least I thought so. Bones said she was a dog and I popped him hard in the chest, which is a good place to punch someone, because there's not much padding there and it hurts. He must've been looking at the wrong girl or something.

Jenny #1 was short and, yeah, she was sort of, well, I think the word is *stocky*. You know, not fat but kind of thick and strong. She looked like the girls on the softball team, and maybe she was, because she didn't go to the Tits. She went to Henderson. That's what she said anyway. I think she might've been a year younger than that, and she'd be a freshman there now, but that was just a suspicion I had, based on the way she talked. It didn't sound like she'd ever really been to Henderson.

Anyway, she had nice brown hair and brown eyes and a little mole or birthmark or something off to the side of her chin, which wasn't gross like it might sound but was actually kind of cool, and it made me think that, you know, somewhere down the line she might understand better than the others what it was like for me. That first day, we just sort of said hi. I mean I said hi, which I did to a lot of girls down there, and she said hi back, which was more rare.

She said it real nice, too, not defensive at all. I stopped when I heard how she said it, thinking I might say something else. She sort of stopped, too, but I couldn't think of anything else, so I just sort of nodded at her and walked over to the snack shack, which wasn't where I'd been headed but was good enough. So that was the day I met Jenny #1, and it's not like we ran off and got married in Vegas or anything, but I definitely filed her away in my memory bank.

I got to the lake a little early the next day, even though it was kind of cloudy. I was looking around for her but, you know, trying not to look like I was looking. There weren't that many people there, and she wasn't one of them, but that's when I met Jenny #2, and this time, I had that second thing to say all lined up: "I'm Mike."

"I'm Jenny," she said, and at this point I didn't even know that the first girl's name was Jenny.

Jenny #2 was pretty hot. Even Bones said so when he got there. She wasn't tall or short, just sort of normal chick height, and she was thin with a little elf nose and big eyes.

"Your eyes are nice," I said toward the end of the day. It was my big Romeo moment, the smoothest thing I'd ever said to a girl. "What color is that?"

"They're hazel," she said.

She looked over at mine but I looked down quick, just enough to cover them up with the bill of my old Sox cap. I wore that cap because it was beat-up and cool-looking and because some of the girls around here were into the Sox, and you could score some points for that. I'm not sure how I did it but I seemed to have racked up some points with Jenny #2. I thought we might make out a little at the end of that day, maybe I'd get my hands somewhere, and just thinking about that, I had to put my towel in my lap because all I was wearing was swim trunks and they tent out pretty easy.

We didn't make out. The most that happened was that we sort of touched knees while we were talking. But it seemed like things were headed in the right direction. I got there early the next day looking for her, and wouldn't you know it, there was Jenny #1. "Dropped something," she said, and sure enough I had, and we got to talking from there. If Jenny #2 showed up that day, I didn't see her.

For four days, Wednesday through Saturday, Jenny #1 and me were more or less coupled up. At the end of the fourth day, we went behind the little climbing wall at the playground. The little kids had gone home by then, and I made it as far as I'd ever made it with a girl. But that's when it went bad, too, because I could see she was making an effort to look at my eye, especially since I wouldn't take my hat off when we were making out. Finally, she came out and said it.

"What's wrong with your eye?"

"I got pinkeye," I said, even though that wouldn't explain the eye, much less the face around it. It was just the first thing that popped into my head, kind of the-dog-ate-my-homework of make-out excuses. She either knew I was lying and didn't appreciate it, or she believed me somehow and just didn't want to be making out with some dude with an eye infection. Either way, that was that. She said she had to go and she went.

I asked for her phone number or e-mail or something before she left, because I pretty much knew she wouldn't be coming back to the lake that summer.

"I'll give you all of that stuff tomorrow," she said.

I knew she wouldn't but I biked down there early anyway. I sat on that climbing wall half the day. Sucks to be me sometimes. It was about two or three days later that I started to think about Jenny #2 again. She was cuter anyway. Cuter and nicer, but I'd blown that, too. I'd seen her a few times over my four days with Jenny #1, and more to the point, she'd seen me with her. What was I supposed to do? The timing was all wrong. God hates me.

But I did get Jenny #2's last name during that one day with her, and it was kind of a funny name, so I had no trouble remembering it. Well, it wasn't funny so much as really unfortunate — I'll just tell you: It was Butts. Even Monday, like eight months later, I still remembered it. And that's when I looked up her profile online and sent her a message.

I did a search by name, and hers came up: right name, right town, right high school. The age said seventeen, but everyone put that so they could have a public profile. Private profiles were for little kids. There was no picture, her page was as crappy as mine, but I figured it was her. So I wrote and sent the stupidest, lamest message in the history of electronics. And now I was in the library to see if she'd responded. I guess that makes me an optimist.

"I need a computer," I said to the librarian. I said it in the way you'd say "I'm a loser," and that's pretty much the way she took it. She asked me what I needed it for.

"Homework," I said, even though I didn't understand why she was sweating me about it. She wasn't even our real librarian, just filling in until Ms. Moreno got out of the hospital.

She gave me a look like she didn't believe me, and I gave her a look like I didn't care, and she said, "Number three is open. Fifteen minutes."

I signed on to my e-mail. There were a few messages but they were all junk. I went to my profile and checked my "pending requests," and there was just one there: Jenny #2. I clicked on her profile and saw that she'd logged on already today, which meant she'd read my stupid message. I felt a little queasy for a second, like someone had just jabbed a pool cue into my gut. She'd read it and she hadn't answered it. She'd seen my friend request and she still hadn't accepted it.

I sat there feeling like a dumbass for a little while, but then I was like, Hey, it's only been a day. And as dumb as that message had been, I still worked hard on it and must've said a few things right. Maybe she was just thinking about what to write back. Like I said, an optimist.

4

After school, I called Tommy's house. He hadn't been around for the rest of the day, and so it seemed like, yeah, they'd gone ahead and suspended him for flipping that desk. There was no answer, which wasn't all that surprising. His mom and his stepdad would still be at work, and he'd probably be at McDonald's or something. I called his cell and it went straight to voice mail. I figured maybe he was talking to someone, so I called back a little later, but it was voice mail again. By then, I was a little surprised. I thought he'd be ready to give me the lowdown, the blow by blow between him and Trever, because it was pretty clear that it hadn't gone well.

Plus, someone would've had to've picked him up from school. They probably would've called his mom down at the town hall for that, and she was always ready to get out from behind that desk. But like I said, no answer, just ring ring ring.

I let it ring, hung up, and tried again. Nothing. Tommy lived over in North Cambria, and Mixer and me were in Soudley. Bones was, too, but farther out, almost in North Cambria. Tommy's house was way too far to walk and too far and too uphill to bike. And there was no one around to give me a lift.

It's funny because, the four of us, where we lived, it was like a line. It was stretched out from the center of Soudley over to North Cambria. It was like connect-the-dots, like four links in a chain, and that sort of made sense. Once we'd met Tommy at the Tits, he clicked right into place with us. He was a scrapper, a headbanger, and just kind of a good guy.

What I mean by that last part was that he was maybe a little friendlier than the rest of us. I don't mean that in a bad way, and not like that was saying much anyway. He was just kind of nicer. Like once we were making fun of some freshman for wearing an honest-to-god sweater vest. (Seriously, not kidding, he was wearing a sweater vest.) But Tommy was like, "Give him a break. He's just doing his thing." Of course, I was just like, "Well, his thing totally sucks," and we all broke out laughing.

Anyway, half an hour later, I got a call from Mixer. "No answer," I told him, and he said, "Same here," meaning he'd tried Tommy, too. But that's not why he was calling. He'd scored a sixer and he wanted to know if I wanted to head out to the house in the woods and help him drink it. I was like, "Damn straight."

We hung up and like two minutes later, there's Mixer

banging on the door. It's a real small town. He was banging hard with his palm. He was hitting the wood part, not the glass, but I still thought he was going to do some real damage this time. He always did that, like he was half knocking and half trying to bust in.

"I'm coming, knock it off!" I yelled through the glass.

The door opens onto the kitchen, and I was right there by the fridge eating a slice of Kraft cheese. I threw the wrapper away, and Mixer stepped back so I could open the door and duck out. He had a paper bag rolled up under his arm, and there were water stains on it from where the beer cans were sweating.

"Hey, man," I said.

"Hey," he said and lifted his chin in a quick nod.

"Hey, bring the Daisy, huh?" Mixer said when we were halfway across the lawn. That seemed like a good idea, so I headed back into the house, shot up the stairs, and grabbed the old junker of a BB gun I'd had since I was ten or eleven. The thing's like a toy: a little brown plastic stock, a Winchester-looking lever to cock it, and a black barrel maybe two feet long.

Mixer was just waiting there in the middle of the yard. There were no cars coming so we crossed the road, him with a bag of beers under his arm, me with a BB gun under mine. No one gave a damn, but because Mixer had the beers, we cut through the O'Learys' backyard instead of walking farther up Route 44 and entering the path there.

It didn't look like anyone was home at the O'Learys'. Their black dog barked at us, but he was penned in and he didn't mean anything by it, just bored. Mixer nodded down toward the Daisy, but I was not going to shoot the dog. Not that it would do any real damage — no way the BB would even break the skin — but that's just stupid. Besides that dog was from the same litter as our old dog, Bullfeathers, and Bully was a good dog, until he got loose out front and got hit by a truck on 44.

It's not that big a lawn and pretty quick we were on the trail. You think of towns getting bigger as time goes on but Soudley had gone the other way. There used to be a lot more to it, back before I was around or even my grandparents probably. There used to be a lot of iron in the ground and people who worked digging it up and melting it down. There were even train tracks, a little railway back here behind town to ship the stuff out on.

The tracks are dug up and gone now, and we were walking on what was left of them, just a sunken dirt walking path, maybe twelve feet wide. People called it the bike path, but you really needed like a mountain bike or something. The dirt was worn smooth in the center, but there were rocks sticking up and sticks lying around and little ditches here and there. It's tough on my ten-speed, but it's fine to walk.

Every now and then, an old path shoots off the bike path into the woods, because there used to be houses back there. Maybe there were a dozen, scattered around like a little town behind the town. Mostly they were pretty beaten down now. A few were leaning halfway over and a few others had gone ahead and fallen down so that the foundations were open to the air, just overgrown pits with rotted boards scattered in and around them. You could definitely fall in at night and break a bone or three.

The only one that was still safe to go in was the house in the woods. It must've been built later or lived in longer or both. Anyway, it had its problems, too. There were gaps in the roof and there was no glass left in the windows. The glass wasn't knocked out, it was just gone. I guess whoever lived there must've taken the windows with them. I'd never heard of something like that before. I mean, didn't the place they were moving to have windows? Anyway, the house had been empty for as long as I'd known about it, which was most of my life.

Mixer and I turned onto the path that led there. The path started out good, but it faded out fast and before long we were pushing through grass and weeds up to our knees. You can't wear shorts out there or your legs'll get all torn up. We were in jeans and boots and sure enough, Mixer was kicking his leg free of something, probably prickers.

"Let go!" he said, swearing at it.

That seemed funny for some reason, yelling at a plant. We laughed a little and then, like that was the sign he'd been waiting for, he decided to dig into the beers. He lifted the six-pack out and tossed the wet bag off into the grass.

It was Meisterbrau, which is not great beer but, you know, still beer.

He popped one out of the plastic and handed it to me. It was still pretty cold and the can was wet so it sort of stuck to my palm. I pressed the BB gun under my other arm so that I could pop the top, then I shifted things around so that I had the beer in my left hand and was holding the Daisy in my right. My finger was on the trigger, but the thing wasn't cocked.

Mixer popped the top on his. He held his open beer in his right hand and we both stopped for a bit to take a big first gulp. When we started up again, he hooked his fingers into the two empty plastic loops and carried the rest of the six-pack that way, hanging low from his left hand and trailing through the grass.

We went down the little dip there and headed into the field that probably used to be the yard, and there was the house in the woods, still standing square on its foundation, its white paint peeling and its empty windows open to the wind. We stood there looking at it and finishing up our first beers. Mixer shook his, to show that it was empty, and I downed the last mouthful of backwash and shook mine, too. Then we both chucked the empty cans toward the house — right at the same second, like we'd planned it — but they were too light and came up short.

The door's around back, or the door frame is anyway. What's left of the door itself is laying on the ground like a big black welcome mat. We didn't bother to go around, just hoisted ourselves up into the empty windows. It was only four o'clock or so, and the sun came straight in through the window and door frames and all the other holes in the place, so that it was almost as light inside as out. The place was full of peeling paint and broken floorboards. There were names carved into the walls, holes punched into the Sheetrock, and empty bottles from older kids who went there to drink.

It's pretty much been worked over at this point, but you could see that it was probably a nice little place back in the day. When I was a kid, I used to think about fixing it up and living there. Now I know there's no way. It's all rotted out. You'd have to knock it down and start over.

Anyway, I walked into the little room that used to be the kitchen. The old linoleum tiles were warped in some places and missing in others. I kicked a loose piece against the far wall. There's a big gap in the tiling that must've been where the stove used to be. There's a thin pipe sticking out of the wall there that was probably for the gas. The stove was in the yard out back now. I'm not sure why anyone would go to the trouble of putting it there, unless they were going to take it with them and changed their mind at the last minute. Like: Oh, man, we can't take this stove. We got all these windows to carry!

I went back into the main room — there are only four rooms in the place, plus the attic and basement — and Mixer handed me another beer. It wasn't as cold this time. I went to lean the BB gun against the wall but just then there was a noise in the attic, a scratchy little sound like *scritch-scritch*. It might've been a shingle falling in from the roof or something like that, but it sort of sounded like something moving.

"The hell?" I said, and I looked over at Mixer.

He was like, "Sounded like *claws*."

So I put down the beer, cocked the BB gun, and fired a shot up into the attic through a hole in the ceiling. I had a couple holes to chose from, so I picked the one that seemed like it was closest to where the sound came from. The Daisy fired with its little *pfoot!* sound, and we could hear the BB hit the roof and bounce back down onto the attic floor. We waited. Nothing. I fired another shot for good measure, then put down the gun and picked up my beer.

After a few sips, Mixer and I sat down, backs against the wall.

"Tommy's in deep, huh?" said Mixer, even though we'd covered that topic already.

"Yeah, what a head case."

"You see Doucheley's face?"

"Nah, I was watching the desk flying across the room," I said, even though the desk really just sort of flopped up and over.

"Yeah, I was watching that, too, but afterwards, Doucheley was like" — and Mixer made this face with his eyes and mouth both wide open. It wasn't exactly how I remembered it, but it was a pretty funny face so I had a go at making it.

"Yeah, that's it," said Mixer.

We sat there drinking for a bit.

"Think he took off again?" Mixer said after a while.

"I don't know," I said. It hadn't occurred to me.

"I mean, it hasn't been that long, but you'd think we'd have heard something from someone. He's got a cell phone."

"Yeah, but we don't."

"He could've called us at home."

"Maybe he's calling right now."

"Yeah," said Mixer, shrugging. "Suspended, though."

"Definitely. Maybe a week."

"He's frickin' crazy. Remember last time, though?"

He meant the last time Tommy'd taken off, and I had to ask which one that was because, truth was, Tommy'd hit the road a few times.

"Manchester," said Mixer.

"Oh, man, yeah. He was crashing with that dude."

"Yeah, good way to get dead."

"Or worse," I said, because there's no doubt there are some sick dudes out there, jonesing for teens and kids and like cocker spaniels.

"Yeah, I think maybe he was a relative, though."

"No, that was the other time."

"Oh, yeah . . ."

"Anyway," I said, "it's a little early to call out the search party. Tommy can take care of himself."

"I guess," Mixer said. "But if any of us is going to get into that kind of trouble, it's him. He's too freakin' . . . I don't know what . . . He's too freakin' Tommy, that's what he is."

Then he threw his empty can against the far wall and opened up another. That was his third, so I reached over and hauled the last one over by the plastic. I wasn't quite done with my second one but I didn't want to get cheated. Technically, it was Mixer's beer, but I knew it hadn't cost him anything.

"Joey hook you up?"

"Yeah."

"Cool."

By the time we finished the beers, it was getting later and the sky was beginning to change. It was maybe dark blue heading toward purple, still pretty early, but the bats came out early in the woods, and we took turns shooting at them. We hunkered down below the window frames, passing the Daisy back and forth and popping up to shoot. It was a game, like we were at war or like the bats might start shooting back.

It's pretty near impossible to hit the things, especially after three beers. They navigate by that sonar, and when you fire, the gun makes that little puffing pop. The sound gets there before the BB does, and it freaks the bat completely. I mean, I think they read that like it's a wall or something. They always dip or dive or swoop and never the same way twice. By the time the BB gets there, it's pretty late to the party and the bat is like two feet away.

Mixer hit one anyway. He was just that bad a shot. The bat dropped like a rock. Its wings ruffled on the way down, but it didn't make any noise at all when it hit. The thing probably weighed like six ounces, and the grass just swallowed it up.

Mixer was just like, "Holy crap! I hit one!"

"Oh, man," I said. "Did you see that thing drop?"

"Yeah, damn."

I was sort of replaying the scene in my head, the little thing just falling to the ground all limp.

"You're kind of a jerk, huh?" I was just busting on him. I didn't really give a rat's ass about the bat.

"Shut up, man," said Mixer. "You were shooting at 'em, too."

"Yeah, but you hit one."

He picked up a chunk of Sheetrock and winged it into my arm. He threw it hard, and it would've hurt if it wasn't for the beer, but I laughed anyway, also because of the beer.

——— ——— ———

My mom still wasn't there when I got home. I was hoping that meant she was food shopping. I went to the fridge and got another slice of cheese, only two left. As I was unwrapping it, the phone started ringing.

"Y'ello?" I said, still chewing.

It was Tommy's mom. She was wondering where he was.

5

Mom got home pretty late, which meant she'd been working overtime down at the bank. She was a secretary, but she put in overtime because they were training her to be like an assistant bookkeeper or something. She said the money would be better, and in the meantime, she got time and a half for the extra hours. It was a little after seven, because *The Simpsons* reruns had just started.

The headlights of the Ford swept across the windows of the front room, where I was watching TV. I got up and went to the hall door, because I figured if she'd gone food shopping I'd go out and help her with the bags. But it wasn't completely dark out yet, so I could see she hadn't gone shopping. She got out the driver's side door and didn't walk around to the other side, just headed straight for the front door.

I opened the hall door and flicked on the outside light,

and she switched directions and came in that way. She looked tired, so I didn't ask her about not going shopping or what we might have for dinner. It's not like she was starving me, so I don't want it to seem that way. I'd just polished off a bag of Doritos while I was watching TV.

It's just that lately it seemed like I was hungry all the time. Forget about snacks in between meals, I needed snacks in between snacks. I guess that's normal. My mom would watch me shovel it in and call me a "healthy, growing boy." I hated that, because it made me sound like a tomato or something, like my only job in this world was to expand, but I guess that's sort of how it works. I was definitely beginning to fill out some, and you don't go from being a skinny kid to a grown man without chowing down plenty along the way.

Anyway, she got in the door and kicked it closed behind her. That was another thing about me getting bigger; sometimes it sort of surprised me how small my mom was. When she moved past me and dropped her purse on the chair by the phone, she barely came up to my shoulder. It seemed like she should still be bigger than me, that she should always be bigger than me, but I guess that was just left over from being a kid and spending so many years looking up at her.

Even without me asking, I guess she knew I'd be thinking about dinner. Like I said, I was getting pretty predictable that way. "Pizza?" she said.

"Heck, yeah!" I said. And that was the good thing about overtime. She must've worked till just about seven, so that's two extra hours, but she'd get paid for three. That's what I meant by time and a half. So now it was like we were going to spend some of that money and get pizza delivered. I was all for food and spending money and any combination of the two, so she walked off to get the menu and I clicked off the outside light and stood there thinking about what toppings I wanted.

We ended up compromising on that, because I didn't like peppers and she thought three meats was two too many. So we got a large sausage and onions, which was awesome. Mom ate slowly. She wasn't super into pizza, which was weird, but Mixer's mom wasn't, either, so maybe that was a mom thing. I knew ordering pizza was more for me than it was for her, and I guess I sort of appreciated that, because I decided to sit down in the living room and eat it with her. Usually, I took my dinner to the front room to eat in front of the TV, but I knew she liked it when I sat at the table. That was definitely a mom thing.

We didn't say much, but it didn't seem to matter. I thought about telling her about Tommy, but what was I going to say, Tommy flipped his desk over and got suspended today and I haven't heard from him since? She knew what kind of kids we were. We got in trouble, broke things. We served detention, got suspended. She didn't need any more reminders of that. We were having some nice pizza here, so why bring that stuff up?

Then I thought maybe I'd tell her how we'd been paid a buck each to carry what we were pretty sure was roadkill. I was going to make a joke about how I was going to start a union to get better wages, like the Roadkill Luggers of America or something. I laughed a little when I thought of that and a strand of cheese blew out of the side of my mouth.

"What's so funny?" she said.

I had a second to think about it while I plucked the cheese gob off the table and stuck it back in my mouth. "Nothing," I said when I finished chewing, because roadkill probably wasn't the kind of thing she'd want to hear about at the dinner table, either.

Mom had seen one of my uncles in the sandwich shop at lunch, so she passed along some family info and I pretended to be interested in it. And that was pretty much it for the conversation. I didn't ask her about her day, and she didn't ask me about mine, because she'd probably worked too hard, and I probably hadn't worked hard enough, and that was just the way it was. Plus, I just wasn't that kid, the one who talked about classes and grades, the one whose mom was hoping he'd become a doctor or a lawyer or whatever. My mom was just hoping I'd graduate, and if it looked at any point like I might not, she trusted me to tell her.

When we finished up, we each took our own plate into the kitchen. She ate a grand total of one slice, so even though I ate a lot, there was still some left over. I figured I'd have one slice later for a snack and another one for breakfast. Cold pizza was one of my favorite things in the world. Cold pizza and I don't know what else. It's kind of weird to think about your absolute favorite things. Summer vacation and my friends, I guess. I liked beer, but to be honest, I was still kind of getting used to the taste. Sleeping in was good. My mom.

The Descent came on cable at ten. It's a pretty good horror flick, plus it's basically all hot chicks, so it's kind of like the perfect movie, if you think about it. I sat there eating cold pizza and watching these creepy crawlers chase after the chicks in the dark. It was a pretty good night, all in all. The one thing I didn't do was read any of that book.

6

"No doubt you are all well into the book by now," Haberman said, meaning the opposite. "What do you think of the opening? Action-packed, wouldn't you say?"

He either meant that it really was action-packed or that it really wasn't. He wasn't asking anyone in particular, and no one particularly felt like answering. Tommy's desk was empty again today, but it almost seemed less strange. He hadn't been home the night before, a fact I knew because his mom was still working the phones this morning, even though I'd already told her I didn't know anything more than she did.

This time my mom picked up. It was the first she'd heard of it, and sure enough, she freaked out. She caught that from Tommy's mom, like the mom flu, which was so contagious it could be caught over the phone. Moms got hysterical easy about their little baby birds. She asked me if I knew where he was, knew anything at all. When I said nuh-uh, she pulled back and stared me in the eyes, giving me that don't-you-lie-to-me look. But I really didn't know anything, and she must've seen that, because she just let me go without another word.

When Tommy didn't show up in homeroom, we figured we knew the deal. The longer he was gone, the clearer it got. He'd hit the road, gone to crash somewhere with someone. It was a family thing now, and his family was eight kinds of messed up. The family he lived with day to day, I mean. Tommy had this endless list of aunts and uncles and cousins and everything else. There were Dawsons all over the place in this part of the state, coming out of the woodwork, and Tommy seemed to get along with every one of them except the ones he lived with.

So we thought we knew, and that was when Haberman kind of climbed into our heads. He almost always paced when he talked to the class, and he was doing that again, but instead of just looking at people at random or scoping out any stray noise, I swear he was looking at me. Over and over again as he talked, and I think he was looking at Mixer, too, and maybe Bones. And then there was what he was saying. "By now you all know of Raskolnikov's crime. How does that rhyme go: Lizzie Borden took an ax and gave her mother forty whacks?"

I hadn't heard that one before, but I knew that Lizzie

Borden was like a historical figure, like Jack the Ripper, so I figured this Raskolnikov guy had offed his mom with an ax, too. I sort of noted that down because it's the kind of thing Haberman would put on a test.

"And it's causing him quite a headache, no? He is in utter turmoil, literally feverish. Does he regret what he did, or does he just fear getting caught? Anyone?"

I looked around to see if maybe someone had read enough of the book to know. You could usually tell. They might not have their hand up but they probably wouldn't be looking down and avoiding Haberman's eyes when he asked the question. Turned out, I was the only one with his head out of the gopher hole, so I got called on.

"Mr. Benton, what do you think?"

"Both," I said, just guessing.

"Interesting," he said, looking at me like we were playing poker. "Murder is a complicated business, wouldn't you say?"

"Yeah," I said. "I guess."

"Indeed. There is the act, the bloody, bloody act itself, and then there is the aftermath. Dostoyevsky is interested in the latter more than the former. He is interested in the actions of the killer only insofar as they tend to illuminate the mind of the killer. To illuminate and to agitate. After all, the act itself, well, he gets that out of the way relatively quickly. It is almost offhanded, his treatment of it. What's he really interested in? Mr. Benton, care to extend your hot streak?"

I shrugged.

"No?" he continued.

He turned around, showing us his back and picking up a piece of chalk.

"He is interested in . . ." and we could hear the chalk scratching and squeaking on the board. He turned around and moved to the side in a little hop, and we could see that he'd written CONSEQUENCES in big block letters.

"And above all," he said, turning back to the board.

This time he wrote, even bigger: CONSCIENCE.

He was sort of worked up now.

"Let's talk about that for a moment, shall we? To Raskolnikov, his acute awareness of what he has done is a sort of personal hell. It *afflicts* him. Is it all in his mind, though? Isn't it just an idea? Like the ones we put on the board yesterday?"

I could still see bits and pieces of those words on the board, where they'd escaped Haberman's sloppy erasing.

"Like crime? Like punishment?" Haberman said.

Like watermelon.

Haberman sat down on the corner of his desk. He was still for a moment, taking the pulse of the class. He did that every once in a while, and when he did, he was like a bug with its antennas up. He noticed everything, the whispers in the back, the movements off to the side, and the energy level of the room, which right now was like a balloon deflating. He frowned.

"Of course, a faraway, long-ago St. Petersburg is just an idea to you as well," he said. "Perhaps that is causing the trouble. Let's say it's not Russia but the United States, not St. Petersburg but right here, in this school. Let's say a murder is committed in this very room, between classes. A student is suddenly missing. It's as if a hole has opened up in the school, but it isn't a hole, it's a murder."

And right there, my ears pricked up. Maybe he was just trying to get our attention, make it personal, but it's a weird thing to say. Haberman was looking off to my right. I figured he was looking at Mixer, because Mixer looked down right then, like there was suddenly something interesting on his desk. Haberman went on, and as he did, he swept his eyes over the class and started looking at me. Standing above us and scanning the room like that, he sort of reminded me of that big, fiery eye from the Lord of the Rings movies.

"That's a problem, isn't it?" he was saying. "Can you see that now? It is no longer a problem for the victim, who is dead after all and beyond caring, but it is a problem for those left behind. As Dostoyevsky writes: 'God give peace to the dead, the living have still to live.' It is a problem for the victim's family. It is a problem for the victim's friends," said Haberman, still looking at me and putting a little extra emphasis on the word *friends*, it seemed to me. Then he broke off his stare, even though I hadn't so much as blinked, even with my bad eye. He swept his high beams toward someone farther over, maybe Bones.

I looked over at Mixer and half mouthed: "A student is missing?" We weren't dense. Plus, it was already sort of in our heads from Bones's joke. Tommy's empty desk was in a line, connect-the-dots style, between Mixer and me. But we weren't crazy, either. Mixer gave me a look like, Is this guy frickin' nuts? I gave him a look back like, I don't know.

"And certainly," Haberman went on, "it's a problem for the murderer. There is a body; there is probably a weapon. It's like a living thing, this problem, a living thing that can stay hidden or can keep extending outward. Say someone, or some ones, help this murderer get rid of the body, aren't they also, in some sense, guilty?"

I looked over at Mixer. He didn't look back. His eyes were far off, unfocused. He was thinking about something, and I knew that it was that barrel.

"And if afterward they wanted to inform the police, the Petroviches of this world, would they be welcomed with open arms or viewed with suspicion? What if they had participated unknowingly, what if they had done nothing knowingly wrong? Would it matter? Would they still be stained by the act, as if dipped in ink? Do appearances matter? What sort of people are they? What sort of person is the killer? What if these unwitting helpers seemed more guilty than the killer?"

The bell rang and Haberman let out a wet little cough. His body slumped down a little. He called out some page numbers, but the class was already loud, collecting their stuff and pushing back their chairs.

"I want you to think about these things when you're reading tonight," Haberman shouted above the noise. "This idea that a crime extends past the moment it is committed. That a man's conscience . . ." but the class was too loud and his voice trailed off.

He took as good a breath as his ragged lungs would let him and shouted, "Just read the book!"

Then he gave up and a little smile crawled onto his face. He looked sideways at me and it seemed like, yeah, I had some reading to do.

7

So I was walking down the front hallway of the main building after school, and god knows I hate the Tits, but the hallways after school aren't so bad. They're empty and open and cleaned and polished. At home, I've got to kick my way through all the stuff on the floor half the time, at least in my room, but after school you can just motor through all this clean open space. You can sort of skate on the tiles, depending on what kind of shoes you're wearing.

It's not like it's a huge thrill; it's just much better than it is during the day. You can pretty much go where you want, and you don't need a pass. That's because the people who stay after school are mostly the jocks, who are outside or in the gym, or the geeks, who are holed up with their clubs. There's detention, too, but then you're shut in the Tank, which is what we call the detention room. So if you're just hanging out after school, it's like you've got the hallways to yourself. You're like 99 percent less likely to run into someone you don't want to. That goes for some senior looking to stomp you or some girl you're avoiding. (And, yeah, it's pretty much always the girl who's avoiding me, but whatever, it could happen.) More to the point, it goes double for some teacher who's been acting like a psychopath.

Before sixth period, I turned the corner heading out of the east wing. I was going fast, trying to get to the library before the sign-in sheet filled up, which I didn't, and I nearly ran head-on into Haberman. He was coming out of the teachers' lounge with Grayson. Now, Mr. G I can deal with, but I'd heard plenty from Haberman for one day. Lucky for me, I was going fast and was past him before he could say anything that'd piss me off. I'm not even sure he saw me. He was already talking and coughing at the same time, and how many things can a man be expected to do at once? Anyway, that's the exact kind of thing you don't have to worry about after school. Most of the time, you turn the corner and there's no one there, just an empty hallway, like in *The Shining*.

The catch is that it's not like you can just leave whenever you want. You've got to wait for the late buses and ride home with the jocks and geeks. Sometimes the late buses are at five, sometimes they're at five forty-five, and sometimes they're even later. It depends on if anyone has an away game or if a field trip's getting back. There's a schedule printed up and you want to check it so you don't get stuck waiting forever. This was Wednesday and the buses left at five, which was fine, because we were staying after to talk things out face-to-face, and it seemed like it'd probably take a while.

I'd just been over at the little roadside place on Route 7, which had the nearest pay phone and was a ten-minute walk from the Tits. They didn't have a pay phone at the school, because if it was official business, they'd let you use the phone in the office, and if it wasn't, they didn't want you calling. A lot of the kids had cell phones. You weren't supposed to bring them to school, but that was like the most ignored rule in the history of rule-making. I would have brought mine in, if I had one. My mom said she wasn't paying for me to have a cell. I'm pretty sure she thought that getting one would magically turn me into a drug dealer. She was half right, though, because it probably would've turned me into a more hooked-up drug taker.

She's clever, too, because if I got a cell myself, I wouldn't have any money for anything like drugs. Those things are seriously expensive when you're not on someone else's plan. It's like fifty bucks a month, minimum. Last winter, Tommy said we should all go in together on a plan. At first we were like, "Jesus, Tommy, how gay are you?" Then it didn't seem like such a bad idea and we looked into it, but it turned out none of us was old enough. Then Tommy talked his way onto his mom's plan anyway. So good for him. As for me, it just wasn't important enough to spend that kind of money on. And what did I really need one for? It's not like I'm a chick.

Except in this case, it would've saved me twenty minutes of walking, round-trip. I'd been deputized, lucky me, to give Tommy's place a call and see if he'd turned up. It sucks when the only one of us with a cell phone is the one who goes missing. I figured his mom would be home, and she was. Just the way she answered the phone — first ring and totally desperate — saying hello twice in like one second, I knew he hadn't turned up. So I hung up. Because what the hell, I was calling from a pay phone.

So I was in the front hallway, main building, like I said, making time. And that's the other thing I wanted to say about the hallways, they have that smell, like, patented. It was sort of like that hospital smell, but without the piss mixed in. I guess it was whatever they used to clean the floors. You really didn't notice it when the halls were crowded, but you couldn't miss it after school. So I got to the courtyard and pushed open the door, and Bones and Mixer were at the table all the way at the far end. There was no one else out there, but I guess they figured this was top secret and the far corner worked best for that.

It was still a few months till summer vacation but it was a nice enough day. I had a denim jacket on but I probably didn't even need it. I could see from here that Mixer had left his jacket in his locker and was out there in just that Nosferatu T-shirt of his that has the hole in the front. I always thought that was kind of gay, having a big hole in your shirt like that. It was just like a little too close to his nipple, which no one needed to see.

So I sat down and gave them the report: "He's not there. His mom's like waiting by the phone."

We started talking, not whispering exactly but not talking full volume, either. We were all talking at once for a little while, because I guess we all had something to say. I'll spare you the play-by-play on that, because there were a lot of lines like: "Is that bleeping bleep-head bleeping bleeping with us?" It's not like I mind the swearing, but there's not much sentence to sentences like that, and we were kind of beating around the bush.

Finally, Mixer laid it out, just to get it out into the open. "I mean, he wants us to think he killed him, right? 'A student is missing' . . . 'it's murder.' Am I reading that right? He's saying Tommy was wrapped up in that barrel, we carted it to the car for him, and now we're guilty, too?"

"He didn't say he killed him," said Bones. "Just that someone did."

"Who the hell do you think he was talking about, dumbass?" said Mixer. "He said it happened in *his* classroom."

Bones shrugged. "Yeah, I was just saying."

There was a red notebook on the table in front of Mixer, the kind with the thin plastic cover and the metal spiral binding. He picked it up, opened it, and started reading. He was doing a pretty good imitation of Haberman's voice.

"'Say someone, or some ones, help this murderer get rid of the body, aren't they also, in some sense, guilty?'"

"That could've been the barrel," he said and sort of tossed the notebook down on the table.

I still wasn't sold on all this, so I said, "Since when do you take notes?"

I thought that was pretty funny, but the others didn't laugh at all, so I could see they were taking this more seriously.

Bones goes, "That is so screwed up. I mean, first of all, Tommy would kick his ass. I mean, it's ridiculous, right?"

But he wasn't telling, he was asking. The question just kind of hung there for a bit. I guess we were all thinking about it. The evidence we had at this point basically boiled down to this:

Tommy, who was missing: It wasn't the first time, but it was still unusual.

Haberman, who was weird: Always had been but was reaching new heights lately.

The barrel: It was the first time Haberman had done anything like that in class.

Whatever was in the barrel: Could've been a deer, could've been a dude, but it seemed like some sort of a dead body to me.

What Haberman said about disposing of a dead body: See above.

What Haberman said about crime being "a matter of opinion": Sounded like something a killer would say.

What Haberman said about a murder in the classroom: Sounded like something a killer would say.

Haberman talking about "the victim's friends" and sort of singling us out: Sounded like something a killer would say if he was also an ass.

So anyway, that's what we were turning over in our heads, all filtered through standard-issue high school paranoia and our natural belief that everything was basically about us anyway.

"Knickerbocker, please," I said finally. It was like this joke expression we had, and the three of us laughed a little, just at how out there this whole thing was. I mean, it wasn't exactly funny, because Tommy really was missing, and even if he'd just run off, that was still pretty dangerous. But the easiest thing to do with something that was bothering you was always to make fun of it.

"Yeah, I mean, it's dumb, but that's what he was getting at, right?" said Mixer. "I mean, he knows we're Tommy's friends, and he's sort of been picking on us. Making us haul that barrel yesterday, and whatever the hell was in there, and today in class, I mean, Mike said he was looking at him."

He reached for his notebook, and I knew he was going to read the line about the victim's friends, and I looked at him like, Don't bother.

"Listen," I said, "I think it's all in the book. I think the Russian dude kills his mother with an ax and maybe like she had some friends. Who saw something or carried something or whatever. I don't know, I'm just going by what he said, but it's a lot more likely that he's talking about the book than about some real-life killing spree. I mean, it's English class, frickin' Homoman. What's he going to do, kill Tommy with that fish club?"

And I wasn't serious about that last part, but as soon as I said it, I got a sick feeling. I remembered that club, hard and balanced in my hand. I remembered how Haberman tugged whatever was wrapped in that blanket out of the barrel, stronger than I thought he'd be. And I remembered the way the blanket moved, all joints and knobs, and come to think of it, the idea of bringing roadkill into class wasn't a big step down in the craziness department from stuffing a body in there.

So now I was finished saying my piece, and it was like the other two were more or less convinced, because they were like, Yeah, that's crazy, dude's in Manchester again, and now I was the one who wasn't so sure. I had the book in my locker, and I had half a mind to go and get it, just to start reading it and trying to match what was in it to what Haberman had been saying. But it wasn't like I was going to sit around with Bones and Mixer reading, so I just sat back and looked over at the glass hallway that runs along the courtyard. I must've caught the movement out of the corner of my eye, because there were three girls walking by.

They were freshmen, I think. There should really be a word for freshman girls, like one without "men" in it, but I don't think there is. Anyway, one of them was kind of cute, once I got a better look. Then I heard Mixer laughing, so I knew Bones was up to something. I turned around and he had two fingers V'd out in front of his mouth and he was darting his tongue in between them. The girls giggled and hurried past us like typical freshmen chicks. Mixer and Bones were feeling better about things now. They were sort of leaning back on the benches like they owned the courtyard, but I was still sitting up and thinking.

When I started talking, they could tell by my voice that I had something serious to say. "I'm not saying it is crazy or it isn't." That's how I started it out, and they sort of looked at each other, because I guess they thought we'd settled this. "But if Haberman did do it, here's how it could've happened."

Then I laid it all out for them: Tommy was in the hallway in the middle of the period. He's in no hurry to get to the office. And there's Haberman. He's got a free period, and he's like, Come in here and help me with something for a second.

I started off slow, just throwing it out there, but as I went on, it kind of fell into place, and I really could see how it could've happened.

I'll sort it out with Trever, Haberman would've told him. I just need help hanging something on the wall, or whatever. Then Tommy's in Haberman's room, just the two of them. Tommy's got his back to him, hoisting a picture frame. He'd be saying, Is this OK? Higher? He'd hang a picture or two if he thought Haberman could really square him with Trever. Then, *bam*, Haberman clocks him on the back of the head with that frickin' club: *Bam! Bam bam bam!* Out comes the plastic sheet and the blankets, like a spider going to work on a fly.

Yeah, I could see that. And by the time I'd finished talking, the others could, too.

8

I didn't do much on Wednesday night. Welcome to my world. It was almost six by the time the late bus dumped me out on the side of the road. The bus just crawls sometimes. I swear, it goes like two miles an hour on the hills. And this area is all hills. On the plus side, Mom'd finally been food shopping. I could smell the Shake 'n Bake as soon as I opened the door. The first dinner after she went shopping was almost always something good: Shake 'n Bake chicken, Hamburger Helper, something like that. It would take a few days until we got to the frozen stuff, but hey, that's why it's frozen, right?

After dinner, I took a bag of potato chips and went into the front room to start reading the book. Mom was probably confused not to hear the television click on right away. That took an hour or so to happen. I put the book down once I figured out who was going to get killed first. I figured maybe I'd pick it up again later.

And I know that an hour of reading might not sound like much, especially with what I was saying before, how I had half a mind to take it out right at school and start reading it there. But there's something you've got to understand: That book is seriously frickin' dense. Thing's like a brick.

There are probably other versions, with bigger type and more pages, but the one we had just crammed the words in there, with tiny type and words out to the edges. The pages were just like all ink. And the writing was the same way: really complicated and hard to figure out. Some of the paragraphs went on for two pages!

Anyway, add it together and you could be reading for a while and not be halfway down the page. And I'm not exaggerating, either. This is one paragraph from the first page, talking about this dude Raskolnikov:

This was not because he was cowardly and abject, quite the contrary; but for some time past, he had been in an overstrained, irritable condition, verging on hypochondria. He had been so completely absorbed in himself, and isolated from his fellows that he dreaded meeting, not only his landlady, but anyone at all. He was crushed by poverty, but the anxieties of his position had of late ceased to weigh upon him. He had given up attending to matters of practical importance; he had lost all desire to do so. Nothing that any

*landlady could do had a real terror for him. But to be
stopped on the stairs, to be forced to listen to her trivial,
irrelevant gossip, to pestering demands for payments, threats
and complaints, and to rack his brain for excuses, to pre-
varicate, to lie — no, rather than that, he would creep
down the stairs like a cat and slip out unseen.*

So there you go, and that was just one paragraph. First of
all, was there a sale on commas? Second, that's a long way to
go to say that the dude was broke and decided to duck his
landlady. After an hour of that I needed a break and maybe
an aspirin. Anyway, I watched *Without a Trace* on cable, and
it sort of felt like part of the same assignment.

I don't know if you've ever seen that show, but it's all about
missing persons. It's not something I watched a lot, but I'd seen
it a few times before, and this one went pretty much like the
others. It starts off, someone disappears, like walks out the front
door and just fades out on the screen. Then this group of FBI
agents, who all seem like they've had way too much coffee and
way too little sleep, go to work trying to find them. They start
by putting a picture of the missing person up on a board.

I tried to remember if I had a picture of Tommy anywhere, like a school photo or something. I didn't think so, but
what the hell would I need one for? It's not like I was going
to forget what he looked like.

Anyway, the thing I liked about the show was that it
seemed sort of realistic to me. I mean, what did I know,

except that it was a little less cute and clever than a lot of other mystery-type shows, and I was pretty sure at this point that real life wasn't cute and clever very often. It's like on other shows, some old lady or flighty dude will string together all of these random clues, like a church bell going off early, some spilled flour, and a cracked picture frame. They'll take all this in, mull it over, and then with two minutes left in the show, they'll be like, Reggie did it! For the inheritance!

And sometimes it was fun to follow along with that stuff, if there was nothing else on, but it just sort of seemed like bull to me. You know how they got things done on *Without a Trace*? They shouted, and if they were really at a loss, they shouted louder. You might think I'm joking, but it'd happened in every show I'd seen so far. Their big thing wasn't collecting weird clues, it was getting people in this little room and questioning them as loudly as possible.

The clues that mattered to them were the ones that mattered in the real world: Who knows who? Who knew the victim, who did the suspect know, who had a grudge or a crush or whatever. They drove all over the place in these sleek black cars, flashed their badges, busted down doors, and hauled anyone like that back to the little room.

Jack was the main guy, Jack Malone, and he was kind of a big, burly guy, and he always seemed about one nervous twitch away from totally losing it. I think sometimes it was an act, you know, to scare the person, but it was hard to tell. I mean, the whole thing was acting, but you know what I mean.

Anyway, he'd get angry and red in the face. He was supposed to be Irish, so that part was believable. He'd yell at the guy, pick up a chair and slam it down, slam his hands on the table, say he was going to arrest him or worse. Or he'd go the other way and lean in real close, still just as angry, like he was barely in control, and whisper in the guy's ear. He'd get totally in his space and go like, Did you kill her?

Sooner or later, the poor dude would crack and tell him something. It wasn't even necessarily something about the missing person. It could just be something that'd lead the agents to someone else who might know a little more. Then they'd haul *that* person in and repeat the whole process. And Jack would be even angrier the second time, so what chance would that person have?

They'd just work their way through everyone who might've had anything to do with the person going missing. And by the end of the show, they'd find them. And yeah, they'd break through the door and rescue the lady or kid or whoever with two minutes to go, just like the other shows, so it was still sort of a fairy tale. It was still TV, when you came right down to it. It just seemed a little more like how things were, that's all.

I mean, cute and clever or angry and loud, how do you think the world works? I think you could pretty much turn on the news right now — or hell, just go through grade school again — and that would give you your answer. And sure enough, I picked up the book again and, right away, this dude killed an old lady with an ax.

9

Mixer and me were out in the hallway before homeroom on Thursday morning. Neither of us had heard anything new about Tommy, and Mixer was like, "D'ya read it?"

I was like, "I read part one."

"How many parts are there?"

"I don't know, a lot," I said. "This thing's got like parts within parts."

He looked a little annoyed, like it was my job to read the stupid thing. Like there was someone with a knife to his balls ordering him not to, for that matter, so I said, "What?"

He shrugged because he probably realized he was being a jerk. Finally, he said, "So?" Meaning he wanted to know if the stuff Haberman said was in the book.

At that point, I really didn't know. It seemed like I'd read a lot, but I really wasn't that far into the book. So I kind of recapped what I did know, thinking maybe he could help me puzzle it out.

"All right," I said. "So, yeah, there's a crime, all right, a murder, but it's not the dude's mom. I was wrong about that. It's this old lady with like a pawnshop in her apartment. He completely offs her."

And as I said that, I realized I was getting ahead of the story, and right away I was in the weird role of feeling like an English teacher or something. I just took a breath and started over.

"So it starts out and this Russian dude Raskolnikov is casing this old lady's apartment, but you don't know why yet. And anyway, the dude's sort of like a stuck-up ass, even though he's completely poor and hard up, and it seems like maybe he's a little nuts, so you figure this dude could do just about anything. Tick tick tick, total time bomb, you know?"

"Yeah," said Mixer. He made a little circle motion with his finger: Move it along.

"But he's having trouble psyching himself up to do some bad thing," I said, "which pretty early on you know is to kill the old lady and rob her little pawnshop. He's all like a commie about it, you know, give her money to the people and all, but he's kind of squeamish about really getting his hands dirty."

"He doesn't want to kill her?"

"No, he does, he's just fagging out about it. So anyway, he meets this other dude who is a total drunk loser, who's like pimping his own daughter."

"There any sex?"

"No, they just say he's pimping her. Or she's doing it herself, or whatever, but the thing is the family needs the money because the guy's a total loser and chicks couldn't work real jobs back then. And so the book goes on about the loser family for a while and then there's a dead horse and a letter from home and none of it seems to have much to do with anything until the dude, the main dude, is walking through a market and he, like, overhears the other chick who lives with the old pawnshop lady saying how she's not going to be home the next night."

"Yeah, so he's going to whack her then."

"Seriously, he thinks, like, the universe is telling him to. So he heads over there the next night, and he's got an ax that he found somewhere on a loop inside his coat, and he gives her some little thing to unwrap and as she's doing that — whack, man! Whack, whack, whack! He chops her up good. But then the other chick comes back, and it's like wrong place, wrong time, and he does her, too."

"That's cold, man."

"Yeah, and she's just like this cleaning helper lady to the old lady, like a relative, who totally didn't do anything except show up at the door and gawk at the body, and this dude — just one shot, whack, she's done, even though he's all like trying to come across as like the people's poet or some crap."

At that point, the bell went off, and we had to get into homeroom. That was fine because that was just about as far as I'd read. Anyway, we were sitting there in homeroom, and I could see across the room that Mixer was thinking about it. I thought that by the time the bell went off he might've come up with something in all that, but when we met up in the hallway on our way to first period, he was just like, "Well, what the hell? Haberman didn't mention any of that stuff."

And I'm like, "Yeah, he's all talking about guilt and spreading stains and getting rid of bodies and weapons and stuff. This guy didn't even really get rid of the bodies, but he did clean off the ax and put it back where he found it. And with the guilt, I don't know yet. He just killed them, but like I said, he's pretty messed up in the head, and I could see him freaking out about it. He's a weird dude and a total bed-wetter about pretty much everything else he does. Like he'll give people money and then go on and on, like, Why the hell did I give them my money for? I think maybe that'll be in the next section."

"Do you think the chicks who got killed had any friends? Remember, Haberman's like, 'That'll cause a lot of problems for their friends'?"

"Nah, I don't think so, but it seems like maybe more people will get killed. I mean, it's just part one and there's already a body count."

"Yeah, maybe he'll kill someone more popular next time," Mixer said, and we both laughed. And then we both really laughed, because there was a 99 percent chance that all this stuff was totally ridiculous, that we were talking about this book for nothing and the only real crime was Tommy maybe getting molested in Manchester. And I said that, too, and so we were laughing even more, feeling pretty good. Then Bones turned the corner, and I was getting ready to tell him why we were laughing, but he was all serious and told us both to shut up.

"What's your problem, man?" Mixer said.

"Throckmorton's here, and he's going to be talking to people," Bones said.

"Throckmorton?" said Mixer.

"Yeah, 'morton," said Bones.

"He want to talk to us?" I said.

"What do you think, dumbass?" said Bones, so that was pretty much a total buzzkill. Sheriff Throckmorton. Not Principal Throckmarten, that we could handle. It was just two letters off, but a major difference. The story was that they were the same family back in the day in Soudley, and that the two names were the result of an old family feud. I've got no way of knowing if that's true or not. I mean, my family has been in town a long time, but that family's like the Founding Fathers or whatever, only no one knows which family that was: Throckmorton or Throckmarten. There's a brook named after one and a street named after the other and, no surprise, everyone always gets confused as to which name goes where.

The other rumor was that the two didn't get along at all, and I heard that one was definitely true, so Throckmorton wasn't here for a social visit.

"Oh, crap," I said, and it was kind of weird, because I honest to god hadn't done anything. None of us had — not recently, anyway — but getting grilled by some dude with a badge and a gun was just not my idea of a good time. Not unless I was watching it on TV. It's like they wrote down what you said and asked you again and tried to get you to screw up. And then it's like you're guilty, even though the only thing you're guilty of is getting confused and saying the wrong thing.

So Thursday schedule, same as Tuesday, and that meant Practical Math with Doucheley first period. And sure enough, not halfway through it there was a knock on the door. Sometimes they call the teacher and sometimes they knock on the door. They don't announce it over the loudspeaker like they did in elementary school: "Will the following students please report to the principal's office." And then the class would start snickering and looking over at you. They don't do that in high school, because sometimes in high school it's serious, and sometimes in high school it's not the principal you're going to see.

Dantley opened the door a crack, and a hand curled around the edge so you could see the fingers. It was a black man's hand, so I knew it was Trever, but I pretty much knew that anyway. The door opened up and no one was surprised when he asked Bones, Mixer, and me to come up to the front. But they didn't know what it was about. At least I don't think they did. Some of the others had been asking us what was up with Tommy, but we were always like, Search me, so they all thought he was just suspended. They didn't know he was missing. They would now, I figured, because Trever called out a few other names, including Max. Max gave me a look like, What's up? But I gave him a look like I didn't know, because Max and me were never that tight.

Then Trever paused for a tick or two and added, real casual, "You too, Dantley."

Man, no one saw that one coming. Trever said, "I'll watch the class till you get back," but Dantley just stood there, a dumb look on his face and his eyes not looking at anything, and you could see that he was confused. His expression was like, *I'm* getting called to the principal's office? Then he turned to Trever with a big question mark on his face, and Trever was just like, "They just want to clear some things up."

It was the same easy-breezy tone but now I could tell that Trever was working at it. I also realized right then that Dantley didn't know who he was going to see, and wouldn't he be surprised when he found out. Throckmorton was the county sheriff. Officially, it was County High Sheriff. Every four years since I could remember, red-white-and-blue signs went up in front lawns saying VOTE THROCKMORTON HIGH SHERIFF. It was like a thing to do to draw a big fat blunt on the sign because, you know, high sheriff.

It didn't matter much, I'd never once seen a sign for anyone else running for the job. Throckmorton lived in Soudley, but he got around. These towns around here were too small to have their own police departments, so it was basically him and his deputies, plus the Staties prowling around to write the speeding tickets.

And that was about as much as I knew about him until it was my turn and I was called into the principal's office. I was surprised to see Throckmarten still in there because of that whole family feud thing. The sheriff had taken over the principal's desk, and Throckmarten was sitting over on the windowsill. They were talking as I walked in. ". . . because he didn't take anything with him this time, didn't pack, not even a pair of socks," Throckmorton was saying, but he stopped talking when the door closed behind me. Throckmarten looked over at me and said, "Micheal Benton," but not to me.

Throckmorton made a sound in the back of his throat, meaning that he'd heard him, and then flipped through some papers in his hands. I was thinking about *Without a Trace*, all the angry questions and accusations and hands slammed on tables.

"Take a load off," he said, putting the papers down on the desk and looking back up at me. And right then, I knew this wasn't going to be like on TV. His voice sounded friendlier than I thought it would, and I had to remind myself again: I hadn't done anything. I didn't know where Tommy was, much less have anything to do with putting him there. There was no reason I should've been feeling the way I was — cornered is the best I can describe it, cornered and under suspicion —

no reason except I was in a closed room with the principal and the sheriff.

There were two chairs on the front side of the desk, and I took my usual one on the right side. I angled the chair to face Throckmorton and sat up straight so I wouldn't be shorter than him. I could feel my shoulders were tensed up and pinching together, so I shook them out a little.

"You cold?" Throckmorton asked, because I guess that looked like a shudder or something. It didn't sound like a real question, though.

"Nah, I'm OK," I said, and then I thought, Am I supposed to call him sir or sheriff or something like that? I mean, I wasn't going to, but I wondered if I was supposed to. He paused, and I sort of looked around. Throckmarten was looking out into the front parking lot through the slits in the blinds. He was wearing a suit, which he didn't always, and I figured that meant he knew the sheriff was going to be there. It was a dark suit and it made me think of my gramps's funeral. The light was coming in through the blinds and cutting him up into slices as he sat there on the windowsill. He wasn't looking at me but you could tell he was listening.

I looked back and Throckmorton was looking at my left eye. He looked down at his papers quick, shuffled them a little, but I'd caught him.

"So I guess you know why you're here," he said, raising his eyes back up.

"Tommy, I guess," I said.

"Yes, sir," he said, but he said it in that hip-hop way, like: yezzurr, and I was thinking: Did he just say that? Because even though that slang was like two years old, it was still slang. I mean, I used to say that. So now I was thinking, What is this dude's deal? Is he trying to be cool and like "relate" to me, or does he really talk like that? He was sitting behind the desk, so I could only see half of him. He had a button-up white shirt on, and it could've been part of a uniform, but it could also just've been a plain white shirt. I tried to remember other times I'd seen him around town, like in the pharmacy or wherever, and tried to picture what he'd been wearing. Was it a uniform, and if it was, would they take it away if he lost the election? I don't think I'd ever seen him in anything else. All I could remember was his face, his gun, and his jacket.

His face was square and fleshier than the rest of him, sort of bulldoggy, and his hair was dark brown, almost black. He still had all of it and I didn't see much gray, but you could tell he was real old, maybe even forty. I always thought of him as kind of a big guy, but up close, I could see that wasn't really the case. The jacket was slung over the chair behind him. It was dark blue and medium weight, and whatever it was made of reflected the light just a little bit.

His gun was out of sight at the moment, but I knew it was a revolver and a little too big, like he'd be shooting at something larger than a person with it. He walked right by

Mixer and me once when we were hanging out in front of the town hall, this was maybe three years ago, when we were still basically kids, and Mixer said, "Magnum." I figured he was right, even though I'd never shot one of those. I'd never shot a pistol at all, come to think of it, just rifles and my uncle's shotgun once.

"You and Thomas, Tommy, are friends, right?"

"Yeah," I said.

"How long have you two known each other?"

"Since start of freshman year," I said. "Going on two years now. Two school years, I mean."

"He didn't go to elementary school with you?"

"Nah," I said. "He's from North Cambria. I went to Central."

Central was Soudley Central Elementary School, which is the only school in Soudley, so I don't know what the central is for.

"Yeah, course," said Throckmorton. "I've seen you around town."

And there was nothing weird about him saying that, I've seen you around, because like I said, he lived in Soudley, but I sort of interpreted it as halfway between neighborly and an I've-got-my-eye-on-you sort of thing. I guess I might've been reading too much into it; I couldn't tell. His eyes were muddy brown and sort of sleepy. People always say, like in the movies, that police have piercing eyes, that they look right through you, but that wasn't the vibe that Throckmorton gave off. He didn't give off any vibe at all. It was like a poker face, which is supposed to be for the criminals, but I could see where it would work for him, too.

"And your friends out there?" he said, looking down at his papers again. "Bonouil and Malloy?"

"Yeah," I said, "all three of us went to Central."

"So Tommy was the new guy?"

"I guess."

"Was that ever a problem, was he an outsider or anything like that?"

"Nah," I said, but he was waiting for more, so after a while I went on. "I mean, it took him a while to get up to speed, but we're all tight with Tommy," I said, trailing off to see if that was enough, but also because there'd been some friction between Tommy and Bones lately, and I didn't think it was a good idea to mention that.

"Get up to speed?"

"You know, like our jokes and stuff."

"Got it. So you guys are good friends now?"

"Yeah," I said. "Like links in a chain."

I just tacked that last part on because, you know, I'd been thinking it.

"Who's closest with Tommy, would you say?"

"Me, I guess," I said. I thought about it some more and nodded, because I was pretty sure that was the case.

"So he'd tell you if he was planning something big?"

"Not necessarily," I said.

"But you just said . . ."

"Yeah, I mean, I'm the closest to him, but that doesn't mean I'm all that close. This isn't like — we don't sit around talking all day. Tommy keeps to himself a lot. We're not, like . . ."

I couldn't think of how to finish that sentence.

"So when was the last time you saw him?"

"When he flipped the desk."

"You didn't see him after that?"

"Not after he left the class. Last time I saw him was when the door closed behind him."

"Haven't heard from him?"

"Nope. Tried to call him. I've tried every day on his cell. Just goes to voice mail."

"You been leaving messages?"

"I've left a few," I said, even though I didn't see why that mattered.

"It's been a couple of days now; do you have any idea where he might be?"

And I laughed, just a little bit, but it surprised me. I'm pretty sure it surprised Throckmorton, too. And the principal looked over from the windowsill. And it was a nervous laugh, too, which was pretty much the exact wrong thing to do. And the reason I did it, and I knew this right then, was because this would be the time to mention Haberman, and this little laugh came out because what was I supposed to say: "Well, Sheriff, he just might be stuffed in the trunk of our English teacher's car"? I mean, I didn't necessarily think he was, but he'd said do I have "any idea," and that was an idea.

I couldn't say it, though, no way. I mean, one, it would sound crazy. It would sound crazy, because it probably was crazy. And two, Throckmarten was right there, and he'd tell Haberman, and those two would have a good laugh over it, and I didn't want to give them the satisfaction. And I remembered one of the things that Haberman had said, too: Who would they believe? And that was spot-on true. I sort of wished I'd read more of the book, so I'd feel better about it myself, but I still wouldn't've said anything. So now I had to explain that laugh away, so I told him about how he'd bused it to Manchester last winter, and how we all thought that was kind of a crazy thing to do. And, you know, I should go to church on Sunday or something, because Throckmorton seemed to buy it.

"Yeah, he's done that a couple of times, I hear," he said.

"Well, not like that. Mostly it's just like a day or two and he's still right around here, like he's got an older cousin in Cambria who he'll crash with if things get real intense for him."

"That Albert?"

"Yeah, I think. He calls him Al. You talk to him yet?"

"He was number one on our list," said Throckmorton. "Says he hasn't seen him."

"You believe him?" I said. The sheriff just looked at me,

and Throckmarten looked over again, so I could tell that wasn't the sort of question I was supposed to be asking.

"No reason not to," Throckmorton said at last. "What do you know about Tommy's family situation?"

And I looked at him for a moment. I'd been pretty much spilling the beans on everything he asked since I sat down. I mean, I figured we both wanted the same thing, as far as Tommy was concerned, so I might as well. But Tommy was pretty touchy about his family situation, as Throckmorton called it, and I understood that. I started thinking, What if Tommy was sitting here and the sheriff was asking the same question about me, would I want him talking? Both accounts would start the same way, in any case.

"It's pretty messed up," I said.

"How so?" said Throckmorton.

I shrugged, but he just sat there, looking at me and waiting for more.

I let out a long breath, and once I was done with that, I was ready to talk.

"Well, the guy who's his stepdad now used to be his dad's boss, and that was a bad scene," I said, and for the first time Throckmorton leaned forward and started writing stuff down as I was talking. I guess that kind of revved me up, because I went ahead and told him the whole thing.

"Like it was like she, I mean, I shouldn't be saying this, but it's like his mom was sneaking around with the guy for a while before his dad found out, and when his dad found out, well, you probably know what happened then."

"Yeah, I took that call myself," said Throckmorton, and I was glad for that, because I didn't want to be the one to say that Tommy's dad beat the crap out of Tommy's mom.

"Right," I said, "and then the guy, his name is Gary, comes over and he wales on him, too."

Throckmorton would know that, too, it would've been on the same call, but I had no problem telling that part.

"So then Tommy's dad doesn't have a wife and he doesn't have a job, either, and for a while, Tommy didn't see his dad, and then it's like, meet your new dad, but Tommy always sort of hated Gary for busting his folks up."

"You think Tommy blames his stepdad?"

"Oh, yeah, totally. I think his stepdad blames his stepdad. He worked real hard to patch things up with Tommy's dad, but that just made it more awkward, if anything. Like I don't think he pressed charges?"

Throckmorton ignored the question. "Is Tommy still close to his father?"

"I got to say not really. I mean, he resents the hell out of his stepdad, but it's not like he seems that cool with his dad. But then his dad's kind of a wreck, and I guess he didn't used to be. I didn't know Tommy back then. I don't think he's dying to live with his dad in that little apartment, if that's what you're wondering. The two are kind of like, what's the word — formal? — with each other, but Tommy'll talk some smack about his dad when he's not around. Which is pretty much all of the time. Not all of the time that he talks smack, but all of the time that he's not around. You know what I mean."

"Yeah, I think I do. I appreciate your help with this."

"No problem," I said. "I'm wondering where he is, too, you know?"

"And you don't have any idea?"

"Nah, wish I did."

"Is there anything else?"

And here, I was thinking about Haberman again, thinking I should just mention it, just throw it out there, that he's been talking about murder and disposing of bodies, because even though there's a murder in the book, there's no disposing of bodies, not yet anyway. And I remembered how whatever it was in the barrel had tumbled out of it like a dead thing. But I just said, "No, don't think so."

As soon as I said it, I thought, Crap, what if Bones or Mixer throw it out there? But I figured I could just say I didn't mention it because I thought it would sound crazy, so then I sort of hoped one of them would.

"All right, then, go on back to class. You can send Mr. Malloy in now."

"You're up," I said to Mixer out in the office.

"Great," he said, and he was looking at me close, trying to

figure out if I'd been raked over the coals. I was going to say something to him, but everyone in the office was looking at us, so we just low-fived as we passed.

When I got back to class, Dantley didn't even look at me. On the plus side, first period was almost over. When we got to English, Haberman wasn't there. Our usual English sub, Ms. Yanoff, was up at the board scratching away.

It was weird because, in a way, I was disappointed. I was waiting for Haberman to say the one thing that would let me know he'd done it or the one thing that would let me know he hadn't. This was getting serious, and I wanted to know. I mean, he probably wasn't going to say something like that anyway, but he definitely wasn't going to say it if he wasn't there. On the other hand, I wasn't sure I had the energy for Haberman's crap after the morning I'd had.

But the first thing I thought when I saw Yanoff up there wasn't either of those things. It was this: Maybe Haberman is burying the body. And also: Pretty convenient that the day Throckmorton shows up, Haberman's nowhere in sight. I mean, him not being there didn't give us any new evidence one way or the other about Tommy, but it definitely made you think. After two days, a body'd be starting to turn, and it would be time to get rid of it, maybe some lime and a shallow grave, like on TV.

Part of me wanted to run down to see if Throckmorton was still around, because I didn't want to take the chance that Haberman might get away with it. But another part of me was like: What kind of an idiot would bury a body in the middle of a sunny day? Plus, Haberman wasn't exactly the iron man of teaching attendance.

So anyway, like I said, him not being there didn't necessarily mean anything, but it gave you some extra room to operate, if you were thinking along those lines already. What's the phrase, enough rope to hang yourself with?

10

So that's where we were. We had questions, the police had questions, the school had questions, everyone had frickin' questions. No one seemed to have any answers. The only thing everyone agreed on was this: Tommy was missing. Throckmorton being there kind of made it official.

Him being gone, it changed things for Mixer, Bones, and me. You could just sort of feel it. It's like if you take one leg off a chair: You can still sit down, but you have to work a lot harder to find your balance and not fall on your butt.

I probably haven't done a very good job of explaining this, but Tommy sort of held us together. I mean, first of all, he was new blood. That can be pretty important when you've been hanging out with the same few people since you were little. He also sort of balanced us out. It's like he had some of the same qualities as each of us. Like he was sort of a scrapper, like Bones, and he was sort of clever, like Mixer. And he was sort of, well, I don't know, whatever the hell I am. I always thought we had a lot in common, anyway.

And I know I've said how he was maybe a little nicer than the rest of us, but he was plenty tough, too. Like he was the one who taught us how to chew tobacco. Or he tried to, anyway.

All four of us were over in North Cambria last summer, because I mean, it's not like it's frickin' Times Square, but there are a few things to do there. Like there's a McDonald's and some batting cages. Anyway, it was crazy hot that day. I guess it was late June, early July. We'd been hanging out in the little town park, the one with the ball field. We were under the big wooden whatever-the-hell-it-is, the thing with the rope grid you can climb up to get to the platform. We were mainly there for the shade, just standing around under the platform, leaning against the posts with our feet in the cool sand.

That's when Tommy told us that he had some Skoal. Mixer was like, "No way," but Tommy was like, "Yuh-huh," and he looked both ways and reached into the back pocket of his jeans.

As soon as he looked both ways like that, I knew he really had it. He pulled a round green container out of his pocket. The word *BANDITS* was printed on the top, and the *A* had a little red bandanna painted on it. It was brand-new and he sort of fumbled with it, trying to figure out the best way to break the seal.

I'd never had chewing tobacco before, and it was pretty clear that Tommy hadn't, either. He hadn't even opened the thing until we were all there, and that right there tells you something about him. While he was trying to pop the top without spilling it all over the place, Bones was saying how chewing tobacco was pretty cool and packed a nice little buzz and how Skoal was like the best kind.

Bones didn't actually say he'd done it before, but that was definitely the implication, you know? That made what happened even funnier.

Anyway, we heard the thing pop open, and I started making lame little jokes. I think I was a little nervous, which is funny because I'd done stuff way worse than chaw. Chaw's weird, though. It made me think of the villains in western movies, like spitting into the bucket from ten feet away.

"All right," I said. "If we're going to do this, we need like cowboy names. I'm Shane."

That might sound a little babyish or whatever, but we were just a bunch of kids under a glorified jungle gym in the summer. We were like a month past being freshmen. And that's how Tommy became Buster and Mixer became Wyatt. Bones insisted on Masterson. I have no idea what ass he pulled that one out of, but it did sound kind of cowboyish.

I was like, "Masterson?"

And Bones was like, "Yeah. Don't wear it out."

I looked over at "Buster" and he started handing out the Skoal. It came in these gauzy little packets, prewrapped or whatever. That was good because I didn't want to deal with loose tobacco, like when a cigarette split. He handed us one each, but Bones said, "Keep it comin'," and he handed him a second one.

The only times I'd ever seen people chewing tobacco in real life was a few of the town softball games and things like that. I was trying to remember how to go about it, like how much to take, how to hold it, where to put it. I just held it in my palm.

"In between the cheek and the gums, ladies," said Bones, still acting like a big shot.

I raised the thing up to my nose for a quick sniff, and it had this minty thing going on. Individually wrapped, mint-flavored . . . The whole thing seemed much less rough than I'd thought it'd be. But I still didn't put it in my mouth right away. I looked around and the others were still holding theirs, too.

No surprise, Bones went first. I guess he was showing off, because he put one in each side of his mouth, like the cotton rolls they put in your cheeks at the dentist. Now, I didn't know much about chewing tobacco, but I was pretty sure that was the wrong way to go about it. That's when I knew Bones hadn't done this before, either. He'd just heard more about it.

He stuck one in the right side and one in the left. He just stuck his fingers in there like he was picking his teeth. For a second I could see his teeth and his gums, and then the tobacco was in and he was wiping his hand on his shorts. The rest of us held our Bandits in our fingers. We were getting ready to join in, but first we were going to watch and see what happened with Masterson there.

He gave us this puffy-cheeked, chipmunk smile, then sputtered something out. I think he was trying to say, "Double dip," but he never got through it. He coughed on the juice and then just froze. His smile disappeared and all of a sudden he had this horrified look on his face. It took me a second to figure out what was wrong: The lump was gone from his left cheek. He'd swallowed one of the packets.

He let out a few short sounds, somewhere between choking and coughing, and then he just started hurling. The first few bursts of vomit came out while he was standing, but by the third, he was on his knees. He was kneeling down in the sand and spewing puke a good two feet in front of him. As skinny as he was, Bones always did like a big breakfast.

We all took a few steps back, and I dropped my tobacco in the sand like it had bitten me. If it was just normal puking, we would've started laughing right away, but this was some intense wretching. You could tell it was painful, and even when it was over, he was still down there dry heaving. His mouth was hanging open like a cat trying to cough up a hairball. So we held it in.

"Jesus," said Mixer.

"Aw, man," said Tommy.

The smell of puke was really strong. If I didn't get out of there, I was going to boot, too, no tobacco required. I couldn't just leave him there, though.

"Damn, man," I said. "You OK?"

He looked up, wiping his mouth with his forearm. It was quiet for a second. Bones spat a few times into the sand and then said, "Damn."

"Dammit, Masterson," said Mixer. "That's a waste of good tobacco!"

"Naw," said Bones, a little smile creeping onto his face. "That stuff sucked."

We laughed, but Bones wasn't off the hook yet. He'd tried to big-time us by double-dipping and then ended up swallowing one of them. We were going to bust his ass, and he knew it. We waited for him to get to his feet, and then we got the hell out of Pukesylvania.

After a while, we walked over to the McDonald's. We put our trays down on the table — just fries and a Coke for Bones, thank you — and it was like a firing line. Enough time had passed and he was feeling well enough and this is where we were going to start cutting into him.

And, I mean, we could've ridden Bones for forever about that, just ragged him mercilessly. But just when we were getting started, Tommy was like, "Same thing happened to Peter J, first time he tried it. Seriously, I saw it."

Peter J was Peter Janklow. He was two years ahead of us in school and seriously, unquestionably cool. He was so cool that the idea that he'd puked his guts out on chaw made it seem like maybe that was the cool thing to do. It was serious cover for Bones.

Tommy didn't have to say that. First of all, I don't even think it was true. But he did, and it sort of let Bones off the hook. Anyway, that was Tommy. And that's what I meant about how he kind of held us together, because Mixer and me, we really would've ripped into Bones. We probably would've gone too far, and he probably would've knocked one of us out. Just like that, we wouldn't have been such good friends anymore.

11

I made it into the library for study hall, but there was a big fat nothing in my inbox. I really thought Jenny #2 might've written back by now. It'd been like three days. But when I saw that she hadn't, I was like, Well, maybe she's just not going to. Actually, it was more like I sort of knew she wasn't going to, and seeing that empty inbox just made it a little harder to pretend I didn't know that, if any of that makes sense.

It was just like I knew the message was pretty bad when I wrote it — I wrote it out in pen beforehand and just typed it in the library — but then I was sitting there, trying to convince myself to hit Send and it was like, Yeah, that's a pretty good message, you know, if you read it the right way. I'll just let you see it, and you can decide for yourself:

Hi, Jenny!

This probably seems like a weird message, but I think it's only weird by real-world standards. Online it's totally normal. OK, no, it's weird here, too. This is Mike, you know, from the lake this summer. (If it helps your memory, I am the one who wore the old Sox cap. It's like my trademark. Also, I am from Soudley and go to Tattawa.)

Anyway, I was out riding my bike and went past the lake the other day, and I sort of remembered how much fun we had that one day (August 2). So anyway, I thought I'd check out your profile. So, you know, hi! I am going to send you a friend request now. I hope you are having a good year!

(I think this is the right Jenny, because of your name and town and stuff. And also because of the kind of music you say you like. If this isn't you, I'm sorry.)

Mike

So that's what I sent on Monday. I know it's not perfect, but it was the best I could do. I read that and I think: friendly, you know, nice. But I could see where a girl could read that and think: stalker. I checked her profile and she hadn't logged on again since Tuesday. I thought about it. Maybe she just hadn't had time.

I went straight home after school. Between Throckmorton, Jenny #2 not writing, and me picturing Haberman out in the woods somewhere with a shovel, it had been a truly crappy day. I was pissed off, stressed out, and tired. I didn't like long phone calls, but I figured I'd have some to make later. I watched some TV and just chilled for a while. Then I headed out to the house in the woods to clear my head and fill my lungs. I'd scored half a pack of Camels for four bucks from Max. He'd pulled up a seat at lunch when we'd been huddling together going over what Throckmorton asked, and what we said, and just sort of sifting through the information. Bones and Max both said they didn't say squat.

Max was like, "I didn't give him anything," like he was being real hard. And I couldn't let that one go, so I was like, "Max, dude, you don't know anything about it in the first place." And having Max there was a pain anyway, because I didn't want to ask about Haberman with him there. If he heard that, it would be all over the school in like a day, not Haberman killed Tommy but Mike thinks Haberman killed Tommy, even though I wasn't exactly convinced of that, but just me raising the possibility would be enough.

But again, Bones said he didn't say anything, said he was in there for like two minutes, and I believe that. I'd seen Bones wall himself up before, just rolling his eyes, shrugging his shoulders, and maybe giving a yes or a no if really pushed. Mixer said he didn't say much, but he answered the family question and mentioned Manchester, too. As near as we could tell, we'd told Throckmorton the same stuff about both, which made sense, since we pretty much knew the same stuff about both. I was like, "Anything else?" And Mixer was like, "Not really."

After that, when Max was talking to Bones about something, I gave Mixer a look like, Really, dude, anything else? And he looked back at me and shook his head no, and he knew what I meant. Like I said, we've known each other for a long time. We started riding bikes together in the cemetery when we were like eight. (The cemetery's a good place to ride bikes, because there's no traffic and the residents are real quiet.)

So it turned out what Max'd been talking to Bones about was half a pack of Camels that he'd scrounged up somewhere. He wanted four bucks for them and Bones didn't have it. Normally, I'd give him a chance to haggle him down, but I was like, Screw it, I really want some smokes, and I bought them on the spot.

It might sound lame, but cigarettes are hard for me to come by on a day-to-day basis. You've got to be nineteen to buy them in this godforsaken state. Soudley's a small town, and not only did everyone behind a counter know me, they like had always known me, remembered me from when I was saving up my allowance to buy candy bars. They knew my mom, knew my aunts and uncles. I didn't have a license or a car, didn't have an older brother.

Mixer and me had tried to make some inroads with this group of seniors who were always smoking out behind the school, but that'd been a disaster. They charged crazy prices, and I think that after our little attempts to get on their good side they were actually charging us more than the others. We couldn't do that, point of pride, you know? Mixer was good at swiping things, but the powers that be were even better at keeping the smokes behind the counter. And Mixer definitely preferred doing his thing in the wide-open spaces out front.

Joey, who used to be cool, wouldn't buy them for Mixer. It's sort of funny, because he'd buy him beer but not smokes. He said they'd kill us slowly. That seemed fair enough to me. Everything else is slow when you're fifteen and living in this armpit of a town, so why shouldn't death be slow and come with a little buzz and a good taste?

Pot and pills were even more expensive. There'd been some pretty big busts just in the year and a half since I'd been at the Tits, and prices had gone way up. The Staties had a dog, which hardly seemed fair. It was a beagle named Snoopy, which was pretty much the perfect name for him, if you think about it. I'm not even sure if he was named after the cartoon or his approach to the job.

They brought that little fleabag into our class in eighth grade at Soudley for like a sort of show-and-tell/public-service-announcement type thing. It was pretty funny, because while everyone else was crowding around to pet him, and his tail was going like a thousand miles an hour, there was that little group of Stantz and those guys hanging way back in the classroom, afraid Snoopy'd get a whiff of their denim jackets.

Anyway, like I said, prices were up. You'd need a job or a big-time allowance. No one wanted to trade with Mixer. I'd heard you could score that stuff at parties once you were a junior or senior and had your license, but I wasn't and I didn't, so that kind of quality high was pretty rare in my life. And huffing, man, that was nasty. I remember coughing into my hand once, and when I looked down, my hand was covered with tiny orange dots from the spray paint. I was coughing paint! That was the last time I did that.

Basically, whether it was the cost, the dog, not wanting to exhale in color, or the fact that there were already kids who were much more into drugs than we'd ever be, that stuff really wasn't our scene. Most of the time, chasing smokes and whatever alcohol we could get our hands on was enough. So when half a pack of Humpies — that's what we called Camels — is three feet and four bucks away from me, it's the kind of opportunity I'll go ahead and take.

Bones came sniffing around my locker later, and I gave him two, so we were cool. And I gave Mixer two for the beers on Tuesday, which didn't leave me much for my four bucks, but what are you gonna do? That was how our economy worked. It was like we were in prison, which is kind of ironic, if you think about it.

I cleared 44 and made it to the trail. I was kicking through the high weeds and figured that was as good a time as any to fire up the first one. And the damn thing was stale as hell. The pack'd probably been open a month. Lord knows where Max found it, probably under a chair somewhere. I'd just assumed he'd gotten the pack new somewhere and smoked the first half. Right then I realized that he'd found the things and must've known they were stale. Now that I was paying attention, I could feel how brittle the paper was, not that fresh almost moist feel of the first cigarette out of a new pack.

So he'd found this old pack and decided that instead of smoking crap cigarettes, he'd turn a quick profit. And even then, it's like, OK, so sell them to some dumb freshman. You're gonna sell them to me? To Bones? Man, that was a good way to get beat the hell down. But by the time I was in sight of the house and lit the second one off the stub of the first, I was willing to let him off the hook, because stale cigarettes were still cigarettes.

Anyway, I was heading up to the house, getting ready to boost myself in the window. I put the cigarette in the corner of my mouth and pushed up the sleeves of my hoodie, and I heard something. It was a low grunting sound, like voices without words, and there was movement, weight being shifted around on the old floorboards. There were people in there and, to show you what a moron I can be, I thought maybe they were fighting.

I took the cigarette out of my mouth and sort of crept up to the side of the window. I slid my head over to take a quick look in, and all I saw was hair, the back of a shirt, and a flash of pale skin. There were two of them, a guy all over a girl, and it wasn't until I ducked my head back out of the window that my brain processed their profiles and told me who they were. I could not frickin' believe it. I took a quick drag and went back in for another look, just to confirm it.

She was kind of leaning up against the far wall, or maybe he was holding her there. There was an empty bottle of Boone's Wine Product on its side next to them, some fruit flavor, which was gay as hell, except for the fact that Bones was on top of Natalie in the house in the woods.

Her shirt and bra were on the floor, and her breasts were just right there, bam. I mean, I got my hands on Jenny #1's once, but she was wearing a bathing suit under a T-shirt, so that even when I got my hand under the shirt, it was still on top of the suit. I'd never just flat-out seen them like that. The only thing in my way was Bones's shirt, which was flannel and hanging open, so that when he leaned in, it sort of draped over her side. That pissed me off for some reason. I guess it seemed selfish. Like, step aside, dude, I can't see.

His left hand was moving over her chest, and his right hand was pushing down at her jeans. She was trying to hold it there, but he was a strong dude, considering how skinny he was, and all of a sudden I wasn't sure I should be seeing this. I kind of got a bad feeling, you know? He was looking down at her, but her head was turned a little toward the far wall. He was doing all the grunting. I ducked my head out again before either of them looked my way.

It was shocking as hell. Like the most shocking thing I'd seen up to that point in my life. I mean, where to start? First of all, I thought Bones was all talk. I didn't think he was actually getting any. Second, I mean, it was Natalie. She was a completely hot property, 100 percent in demand. Tommy had called dibs like the first day we met him, and it was like, sure, whatever, because it didn't seem like any of us had a shot with her anyway.

And Bones was probably the one with the longest odds against him; at least that's what we thought. Bones is a cool enough guy, but he's just a dirtbag. When I call him that, I sort of mean it as a good thing, but that's not how most of the girls in our school would take it.

And that was especially true of Natalie. She was tall and pretty and just sort of seemed better than the rest of us. She looked like she should be somewhere other than our little dump of a high school, and she'd definitely had a lot of practice shooting guys down. Like a lot of the hottest girls, she was just this side of being kind of weird-looking. Like how you see models on those shows and they are all stretched out in one way or another. *Exaggerated* is the word. Like one will be six four and another will have a head that's too big for her body. With Natalie, it was her legs.

She was almost as tall as me, and even so, she was still

mostly legs. I guess it was possible she'd grow into them, but that would make her like seven feet tall. Her eyes were a really pale, washed-out blue, almost gray, like vampire eyes. It seemed like if you turned out the lights, they might actually glow. She had dark hair and kept it short, which not many of the girls were doing, so it seemed sort of unusual and cool. Not that any of us spent much time looking at her hair. If she was walking toward you, all you saw were those long legs and laser-beam eyes. I'd seen guys walk into lockers looking at her.

And, I mean, there were some other truly hot girls in the school but, you know, not many. She was another one who the teachers were always badgering for not "living up to her potential." But I think a lot of them just wanted to help her out after school, if you read me.

All that said, and here she was basically getting mauled by Gerard freakin' "Bones" Bonouil. I mean, Bones was my friend, but he was also pimply, skinny, not especially funny, and not all that nice. And Bones was Tommy's friend, but he was kind of screwing him over. I sort of had to wonder, and not for the first time this year, what was up with him. I mean, yeah, he was an angry dude. We've covered that territory, but he'd always been a decent friend, and he'd always had some kind of reason for the things he did. These days, it was getting harder to figure out where he was coming from. I sort of figured it was because he was older — sixteen to our fifteen — but it was hard to say exactly. I mean, we'd all changed a lot.

It's not like he couldn't get with Natalie. If he had a shot and Tommy didn't, Tommy would have to step aside, but he should've cleared it with him beforehand. He was crossing a line. It was like in October, when he beat the living hell out of that kid, that Adam what's-his-name. And I mean, Adam was a freshman and a weird one. Everyone picked on him some, but we came across him alone by the pizza place, and Bones just went to work. If Adam did anything to provoke him, I didn't see it, and he definitely didn't do anything to deserve what he got. He was a mess afterward. He had a bloody nose that left a thick red snail trail clear down the front of his shirt.

When it was all over, I was like, "Dude, WTF?"

But Bones just shrugged and said, "I hate that kid."

That's not really a reason for a beating like that, so I said, "Yeah, well, I hate Monday mornings. It doesn't mean I'm going to beat the crap out of them."

"You would if you could," he said, and I ended up laughing because he had me there. It was still like that with Bones; one minute you think you should be getting as far away from him as possible, the next, he was the same old jackass you'd known for years. It just felt like the ratio was shifting, like he was getting a little worse, is all. Maybe that's just what sixteen was like, but I sort of hoped not. One way or the other, I was pretty sure I wouldn't end up laughing about this one.

I felt a sharp, stinging pain in the first two fingers of my right hand. The cigarette had burned down to the filter. I swore under my breath and shook it loose.

I put the two fingers in my mouth to soothe the burning and stood stock-still, like I was hunting and a buck had just stepped into the clearing. Did they hear me? It was under my breath, but only sort of. I had an urge to make a break for it, even though I hadn't done anything wrong this time, either.

I mean, yeah, I'd gotten a free show, but this was like a public place, not their house and not mine. It didn't even have glass in the windows. I could just stick my head in the window and say, "Hey, Bones, when you're done, you should know those cigarettes I gave you are stale." But for whatever reason, it felt like skulking around was the way to play this, so I was standing real still and listening, but Bones just kept on grunting away, and Natalie was just sort of mumbling something.

I thought I'd better take another look anyway, or maybe, you know, I just wanted another look. I sort of hated myself for having a boner. It just seemed kind of pathetic, standing outside with a burned hand and an erection, but there I was, sticking my head back in for another peek.

Natalie was on her back looking up at the ceiling now, not at Bones but just past him. The look on her face wasn't at all what I was expecting. She wasn't into it, and she wasn't angry, which I'd figured were the two possibilities. She looked as bored as she did in class. Her giraffe legs looked useless and a little sad, lying open on either side of Bones. There was sweat on the side of his face, and I looked down and I could see that her jeans were undone now and he had his hand most of the way inside. His wrist was bent back in a way that looked uncomfortable but, all things considered, not too bad. I bent my wrist and sort of imagined my hand there. I looked back up, and she was looking right at me. She didn't scream, didn't do anything, just looked me in the eye.

I figured I was caught, flat busted. My first thought was to duck down, but she'd already seen me, and Bones wasn't looking at anything except her. Her left arm was sort of propped against his chest, half pushing at him and half useless, and that arm told me pretty much everything I needed to know about who was driving that train. I looked at the arm, looked at her, turned around, and left.

I'll be honest, that was the first time I'd seen something like that. It was pretty heavy. It wasn't with me, of course, but it was still the first time I'd seen anything remotely resembling sex anywhere other than on TV. In a way, her looking at me like that was kind of hot. I mean, it sort of involved me, if that makes any sense. But it was messed up, too. Her expression, really her lack of an expression — it was like she barely noticed me. It was like she barely noticed him, for that matter. There was that bottle of Boone's, but Boone's didn't fog your eyes over like that. What was going on in there, it wasn't the sort of thing you necessarily wanted to be around.

I turned around when I reached the top of the little slope that led down to the house. I bent down, fingered through the grass, and picked up a rock about the size of my palm. I winged it at the old beat-up roof. For a second it looked like it was going to make it into one of the holes, but it hit right on the edge and bounced away. I watched as a shingle tipped and fell into the dark gap of the attic. I kind of hoped they heard.

It wasn't much of an effort on my part, I guess, but whatever was going on in there was their deal. I don't know what she was thinking, meeting him there like that. But again: Not my deal. I'm no hero. When I was a kid, I wanted to be Wolverine — kind of a tough-guy hero — but by now I knew I wasn't even that.

You know before, when I said that Bones had to be pulled off people in fights, like he was a dog and you had to grab his collar and maybe a fistful of neck, too, and pull him clear before he could do some real damage? Well, that's a weird thing to realize about someone you've known since they were a little kid, but it's even weirder to realize that you might not be the guy to do it. I mean, we were growing at about the same pace — he was taller and I was wider — but I couldn't match his intensity anymore, couldn't even understand it sometimes. What was so important about anything around here that you had to fight for it? We were still living at home in this crappy little town. I guess I was just sort of headed the other way from him. I was biding my time until I got my license, finished school, got something of my own, and he was still defending his turf like a schoolkid. He was defending it like it was shrinking, fighting over scraps.

You think I was going to go in there and pull him off that girl? Yeah, he might listen to me. He might also tear off my arm and beat me with it. That was a two-man job, and Mixer wasn't around. Yeah, I felt bad for Natalie, for what I was pretty sure was happening in there, but I hardly knew her. I'd never once talked to her one-on-one — like she'd even stay put for that — and Bones and me, we had that history. Add it all up and it amounts to the same thing: not my deal.

Once I reached the thinning grass at the mouth of the path, I took out the matchbook and lit up another crumbling Camel. Only a few left.

12

So obviously I had a lot to think about on Thursday night. I talked to Mixer, but I didn't tell him about Bones and Natalie. That was too big a bomb to drop over the phone, so I just told him there was something I had to tell him before homeroom and left it at that. I couldn't even bring myself to call Bones about Throckmorton and all that other stuff, and there was no way I could concentrate on reading more of the book. Instead, I watched *Without a Trace* again and *The Mummy* for like the twenty-fourth time.

I was drifting off to sleep and I was thinking about, well, you know what I was thinking about. The Kleenex were still crumpled up in little balls on the floor next to my bed, but I was still thinking about Natalie and Bones. Like, if that was a one-off thing or if he'd been hitting that for a while. I mean, she pretty much seemed like a passenger on that ride, but she was there with him, and that had to mean something. Then I was thinking, because it's like sometimes I don't sleep that well, and I was thinking about how Bones and Tommy hadn't been getting along lately, and so it was like the light-bulb went on.

All of a sudden I had a whole new idea about what might've happened to Tommy. I mean, hell, I might take off, too, if I'd been sniffing after the same girl for years and Bones beat me to it. I mean, Bones was nobody's idea of Brad Pitt. He wasn't even like some actor's normal-looking brother who ends up on made-for-TV movies just because of who his brother is. No one would watch Bones, not even on TV. The point is, I could see where that'd burn Tommy up.

That'd explain why he flipped the desk, too. Natalie and Bones were both in that class, and he wasn't going to be able to say three right — and you just knew Dantley'd make him repeat it — and maybe they'd both be back there laughing at him behind his back. A guy'd do some crazy stuff to avoid that. And once he'd done it, maybe he just needed to cool off for a while. Or maybe he was off hunting for a .38. Anyway, sleep was coming on and that seemed to make as much sense as anything else. I figured I had to talk to Bones, to corner him and get it out of him, so I made like a mental note and hoped I'd remember it when I woke up.

It came back to me about the second time I hit the snooze bar and that was enough to get me out of bed. Plus, it was Friday. TGI-frickin'-F, people. I got dressed, scarfed down some cereal, and went out and waited for the bus. It was a warm morning, still sort of gray, and I could see fog up on the mountain, hanging there like shampoo in the trees. The yellow dog pulled up and I climbed on, and Mixer was sitting on the seat over the wheel hump.

He didn't always take the bus, because sometimes his dad dropped him off on the way to work, if his dad was working down that way. All things considered, this was a good day for him to be there. Bones's house was at the tail end of the Cambria bus route, and that was fine, too, because Mixer and I had stuff to talk about without him. It's bumpier when you ride over the wheel hump. That's why people like it. But it's noisier, too, so we could talk normal, without worrying about anyone else hearing.

I told Mixer what I'd seen, and when I told him about that, plenty of people heard him. I think the bus driver even heard, but there's only so much you can read into "No freakin' way!" so that was fine. He got quieter when I told him my new idea about why Tommy might've taken off. Mixer smelled like cigarettes, so I knew he'd smoked at least one of his Humpies out at the end of his dirt driveway waiting for the bus. It's not something I'd do, because if the bus arrived early, you'd have to crush it out on the ground and that was a waste.

Anyway, Mixer agreed that it might've lit a fire under

Tommy's ass, and he was sort of mad, too. It hadn't occurred to me to be all that mad about it, but Mixer was like, A) It's kind of a crappy thing to do to Tommy, bad as he had it for Natalie. And I was like, Yeah, like you wouldn't've done the same thing if you had the same chance, but Mixer was having none of it.

He just went on and was like, "B) If that's what happened, then Bones should've clued us in. We're all sitting there talking about Haberman, and he's like, 'Yeah, what if?' Meanwhile, he knows full well where Tommy's gotten off to."

But Mixer wasn't really thinking this through, so I had to call him on it. "Yeah," I said, "but he might not've known. Maybe he didn't even know Tommy knew."

I wasn't completely sure that sentence made sense, but I was sure about the next one. "And anyway," I said, "he wouldn't've known where Tommy got off to, just why."

"Yeah, well, he should've told us that," said Mixer. "And it was still a dickhead thing to do."

"No argument there."

"All right," said Mixer, and you could hear he was making an effort to calm down, "we'll catch up with him after homeroom. Might as well get his side of the story."

"He better not dick us around," I said.

"Once he knows you saw, he won't try to feed us any bull," said Mixer. "Man, Bones. I still like him and all, but I'm definitely beginning to wonder about that guy."

"Yeah, I wonder how he got Natalie to look at his scrawny pale ass without running in the other direction."

Mixer just shrugged. "Maybe she was wasted."

"Could be," I said.

— — —

We caught up with Bones at his locker. At first, he was like, "You saw me? You frickin' saw me?"

I was like, "What? I go out there all the time, and you forgot to put the DO NOT DISTURB sign out. Looked like you had your hands full, so whatever."

"How long were you there?" he said. "How much did you see?"

"Enough," I said.

"Forget about what he was doing there or how long he stayed, he lives across the damn street," said Mixer. "What the hell were you doing there?"

And so he told us. I'll give it to him, too, either he was a smooth operator or the truth just happened to hang together nicely. And since I knew he wasn't smooth, I went ahead and believed him — except for the parts where I knew he was lying. The way he told it, he just lucked into it. He said he biked down to the trail and walked to the house from there, and I knew he did that sometimes. He said Natalie was already there, pretty much blotto and totally good to go. He said she had another bottle, too, a fifth of Southern Comfort.

"Damn," said Mixer, "what'd she do, open a package store?"

"Seriously," said Bones. "Wish she'd saved me some."

He said it was her idea, that she was talking dirty from

the start. He was lying about that part. Forget about talking dirty — it looked like she was barely able to talk at all. There was no fifth of SoCo there, not unless she'd swallowed the bottle, too. I remembered her eyes. She'd popped something — Percocet, Hydrocodone, or one of those — something prescription and strong.

I didn't bring it up, didn't call Bones out on that point, because if that's what happened, well, they've got a word for that, and it's not the sort of word you want to hear or say. Not with Throckmorton sniffing around. For all I knew, I could be sitting in front of him in twenty minutes.

And anyway, the fact of the matter was that he hadn't been doing anything with Natalie while Tommy was still around. I believed him on that part. He'd stumbled into this one. She'd gone there to chase some pills with some crappy fruit-flavored fake wine and to be out of it for a while, and it was just bad timing. The boogeyman had shown up. I wondered what that must've been like, to be almost out and to have to try to claw your way back. Like being too far underwater, maybe, and not knowing if you were going to be able to make it back to the surface in time — I remembered her long legs lying open — not even being able to kick.

"I was totally gonna tell you guys," Bones said. "Give me a break, it's not even first period."

"Yeah, I'll bet," said Mixer. "You couldn't keep this to yourself if you tried. It's incredible."

"Unbelievable," I said, and I'd chosen that word special.

13

At this point, we were pretty worried about Tommy. He'd never been gone this long, and the police had never been involved before. I'd told the guys what Throckmorton had been saying — about Tommy not packing this time, not even a pair of socks — and we all figured they knew more than that.

Now we knew that Tommy hadn't skipped out because of Bones and Natalie. My little one-day brainstorm had fallen apart, and we were right back at square one. There were only two people on square one, two people we figured could be responsible for Tommy going missing. Tommy himself was still the odds-on favorite, but Haberman had been coming on as the days went by. And he definitely kept himself in the race in English class.

He was watching me as I walked in and had that same

creepy smirk on his face, and as much as I'd been glad to spend a few hours with a less-crazy idea about what might've happened to Tommy than that Haberman stuffed him in a barrel, I still slipped back into thinking it pretty easily. It was how he acted, what he said, him looking at me, same as before.

I'm just going to give it all to you, full-blast, both barrels, so that you can see the kind of crap we had to wade through in that class. Day in, day out, it was pretty much like this, so much hot air that the room would float away if it wasn't nailed down, but there was more to it than that, like I've been saying. Separating what he meant from what he said was getting tougher and tougher so, you know, here's all of it. Maybe you can figure it out.

He didn't mention where he'd been on Thursday, if he'd been sick or what, and except for that hacking cough, he seemed healthy enough to me. We weren't even all sitting down yet, and he launched in. When Haberman did that, it meant he had more to say than there were hours in the day, and under normal conditions, that sort of cut both ways. On the one hand, it meant we'd have to hear him talk for the full forty-five, but on the other, it meant there wouldn't be many questions, no real reason to stay tuned in. But these weren't normal conditions, because if you thought the guy talking might've killed your friend, then you'd pay real close attention. Maybe you'd even write stuff down.

"I'd like to skip ahead a bit to part three, chapters four and five, the scenes in which Raskolnikov first meets Porfiry Petrovich."

And I opened my book, because I wanted to see if the stuff he was going to talk about was really in there. I didn't recognize the name from the part I'd read, but I knew all the names were like that, like Andrinokov Andonovyanoffakov or whatever.

"Page 243, for those so inclined," said Haberman. I'm sure he was looking at me, but I didn't look up, and even though it looked lame, I flipped to page 243.

"Notice the feigned indifference in his phrasing, as Raskolnikov asks his friend Razumihin, 'You know that . . . what's his name . . . Porfiry Petrovich?'

"But of course he does; Porfiry is his friend's relative. Raskolnikov is acting here, but why? Why would he conspire to visit the man in charge of investigating the murder he committed, the crime that has seemingly been driving him to the brink of madness for most of the book?"

Haberman was always saying things like "the brink of madness." Anyway, he wasn't really asking us a question here. He was going too fast to stop himself from answering.

"He wants to retrieve his pawned trinkets, certainly. That is the literal explanation, but there is a clue. 'I know I ought to have given notice at the police station, but would it not be better to go straight to Porfiry?'

"Now, recall, the last time he was at the police station, he fainted and nearly gave himself away. He hardly wants to repeat that, and here is an opportunity. Why go to the police station, surely the last place a murderer wants to be if he can help it? Why go there, when you can go to the relative of your best friend, with your best friend in tow? Certainly seems like a better approach. Wouldn't you say so," and here he paused, like he was picking the name out of a hat, "Mr. Kaeding?"

And Jerry was like, "Yeah, sure."

"I am sorry to say that you are wrong, Mr. Kaeding," said Haberman. "I set a bit of a trap for you there. Raskolnikov is walking into one, as well. He is walking right into the spider's web, as it were, and he begins to understand that before he even arrives, before his feet begin to stick to the filament, because his friend describes the inspector as 'intelligent,' 'skeptical,' 'cynical,' and most alarming of all, 'very, very anxious' to meet him."

I turned the pages and found the part he was talking about. So far, it pretty much checked out.

"'On what grounds is he anxious?' says Raskolnikov, and you can imagine the alarm in his voice. But his wits have not deserted him entirely, not yet, anyhow. He teases his friend, makes fun of how Razumihin had doted on the sister, Dounia, so that when they arrive at the inspector's apartment, they are laughing, laughing loudly, unconcerned and having, it might seem, a grand old time. Certainly, that is how Raskolnikov means it to be taken.

"And yet it is all very serious. He has entered the chambers of his great nemesis now, his Grand Inquisitor, if you will, and when the door closes behind him, well, how must that feel?"

And now he really was asking: He asked Mixer. "Mr. Malloy, how do you suppose that would feel? You are guilty of something, something quite serious, and there you are, in a closed room with a police officer. You find yourself answering questions, being watched. How would you feel under those circumstances?"

And of course, he knew — everyone knew by now — that Mixer had been "under those circumstances" just the day before. Mixer and the rest of us, in the principal's office, behind that big thick door, getting quizzed and eyeballed by Throckmorton. And if that part was true, then it was like, what about the first part, the part about being guilty of something? And it was back to that spreading stain crap he was saying and disposing of the body. And Mixer could put all this together as fast as I could, and he wasn't answering.

"It wouldn't matter if you hadn't done anything," I said, just to get him off Mixer's case, before Mixer said something stupid.

"Why, Mr. Benton," said Haberman, wheeling around, "what a strange thing to say. But of course he's guilty."

And now I was the one not saying anything, because I was talking about Mixer, and Haberman was back to talking about the book. I just shrugged. His eyes were intense, staring at me like I was food. It weirded me out and I looked away a little, just over his shoulder.

"And thus, the interrogation begins," said Haberman, launching back into it. "He sits him on the couch with 'that careful and over-serious attention which is at once oppressive and embarrassing.' And at first, Raskolnikov does quite well, doesn't he, Mr. Benton?"

"Sure," I said, not committing to meaning it and still not looking at him.

"But he does: 'in brief and coherent phrases Raskolnikov explained his business clearly,' but, and here is the key point, he doesn't stop there. He just can't. Raskolnikov simply cannot shut up. He is in a room with not one inquisitor but two, and he keeps on talking."

And I was thinking, Throckmarten and Throckmorton, and how I'd talked so much more than the others. How I'd been in there longer, talked more, and how the others had all, whatever they said, sort of noticed that.

"And he botches it: 'I haven't been well' one moment and 'I am quite well, thank you' the next. He panicks and flatters Porfiry and then tries to explain his flattery. And suddenly, it's not going well, not going well at all. The noose seems to be tightening, but even at this point — the exchange on the second half of page 253 — he has said nothing especially damaging. He is just acting strangely, as he had with Zametov the day before, Zametov who is also in the room now, a sort of quiet, lurking presence."

And here I thought of Throckmarten, how I'd seen him and Haberman talking and laughing a few times, how I once saw the two of them drive off in Haberman's car. The top was down and Throckmarten was in the passenger seat, while I was sitting there fogging up the window of the slow-ass, rust-bucket bus.

"No, what really gets him into trouble are his *ideas*," said Haberman, and he drew the word out, like eye-deeeeeyas. "The question comes up, 'Whether there is such a thing as crime.' You remember, we discussed this, the barrel, the words on the board: *crime* and *punishment*. Are they real things or just ideas, matters of opinion?"

I looked at the board, but the last traces of those words had been wiped away.

"Raskolnikov sees nothing strange about this. It is, he says, 'an everyday social question,' and one about which he has some very strong — and unusual — opinions. Does anyone know what they are?"

He was about to plow ahead, but someone actually spoke up. I turned around, and it was Bridgit, sitting next to the empty desk where Natalie usually sat.

"Excuse me?" said Haberman, because he hadn't quite heard what she'd said, either.

"The article," she said, slow and careful.

"Yes!" Haberman shouted.

I swear he damn near creamed himself.

Bridgit was just kind of in the middle on everything, not too popular, not too good-looking, and not too cool, but not un- any of those things, either. You really only noticed her when she did something like this, something unexpected. She'd actually read the damn thing. I looked down at my book. It was open to page 256, and she'd read what came next. I mean, a lot of books aren't even 256 pages total.

Haberman walked toward the back of the class and, for a while, he was talking to Bridgit, just the two of them. There was an article that this dude got printed in a magazine. It was about crime and how it was OK for some people and not others, and this cop had read it. And it's like, Yep, that's a pretty good way to screw yourself over, writing something like that, especially if you're going to follow that up by going out and actually killing someone.

But Bridgit, even though she'd read that far, stopped being interesting to him, and he walked back toward the front of the room. It was like he couldn't stay away from the three of us for long, so he came back. "And his ideas, quite remarkable. That some people are ordinary, the masses, the cattle in the field," he said, and he drummed his fingers on Bones's desk as he passed. Bones looked at Haberman's back with a world of hate in his eyes. "And that some people are extraordinary, above society's little rules. Destroyers, he calls them, destined to break laws on their way to creating new ones."

I flipped through the book and there it was: Starting on

page 259, the words *ordinary* and *extraordinary* dotted the pages. You just knew which category Haberman put himself in.

"We will talk about that more on Monday," he said, and since his back was still turned, Max took the opportunity to let out a groan. "Much more," said Haberman, as he turned around to face us again.

"But what is crucial here, is that Raskolnikov, against all common sense, allows himself to be drawn into this discussion, to tell two police inspectors that he considers some people to be above the law, licensed by 'their conscience' to, as he puts it, 'wade through blood' — to wade through blood! What on earth would make him say such a thing, even if he believed it?

"Is it pride, intellectual vanity, or is it, on some level, a desire to be caught? Certainly, he has come close to confessing at a number of points. And then, too, he is not even sure they suspect him."

My head was sort of swimming. All this stuff was in the book; it didn't have to be about Tommy, about Throckmorton, and sometimes, like now, it seemed like it wasn't.

"Raskolnikov is thinking: 'All their phrases are the usual ones, but there is something about them,' and it is a panicked thought. 'Why do they speak in that tone?' he wonders."

And it's funny, because I knew just the tone he meant.

"So maybe, before he is drawn into that last discussion, into issuing his little treatise on crime, he is in the clear. If that is so, what is the book saying here, what are we to take away from it?"

By now, the whole class was watching the clock, waiting for that last tick that would set the bell loose.

"Is it that it is not only Raskolnikov's actions but also his ideas that have gotten him into trouble? Ideas, after all, can be very dangerous things. Say you had done something very bad, but that because of lack of evidence or simple good fortune, you were liable to get away with it. Why, then, would you complicate matters by sharing wild ideas on the topic with anyone, much less the police?"

I was looking down, stacking my books, but I figured he was looking at me when he said these things. If he was, this is what he was saying: Don't talk to the cops, don't share any "wild theories."

The bell rang and he called out more page numbers, a big chunk because it was the weekend. I looked over at Mixer as I stood up. He was still steaming from that what-if-you-were-questioned-by-the-cops thing, and the look in his eyes was like, Screw this. I was still thinking about the don't-share-wild-theories stuff. We were sick of this crap. We couldn't figure it out. Was he talking about Tommy or wasn't he? Wednesday it was like he definitely was, and today it was just like, Well, he could've been. Asking Mixer about the cops like that was fuel for the fire, but even that was sort of in the book.

We'd just lost one theory about what might've happened to Tommy when Bones squirmed off the hook, and now it seemed like this one might be getting away from us, too. We needed some straight answers, and soon, before Haberman crawled back into his hidey-hole and became just a teacher again. Mixer stopped at my desk and he nodded toward Haberman's back, like, Yeah, we've got to settle this. I looked over at Bones and that crazy bastard was up for anything.

14

I woke up late on Saturday morning. Little bits of the dream I'd been having skittered out of my head like quick, slick bugs. There was a hole in the roof of the house and leaves were blowing in, piling up in the corner of the room next to mine. Then I was in some kind of house made out of glass, maybe a greenhouse. I was chasing someone and was full of bad intentions. There was a shotgun leaning up against the wall. That was all I could grab before it all tumbled out my ears.

Sunlight was streaming in my window, and I could hear the cars going by out on Route 44. I wiped the gunk out of the corners of my eyes and checked the alarm clock. It was almost ten, which was like a bonus. I almost never slept that late or that well.

One of the many crappy things about having to get up

early for school five days a week was that, even when I didn't need to, I usually woke up early. My body was just trained, I guess, and it was getting worse as I got older. Last summer vacation, it was July before I started sleeping much past eight.

The house wasn't big, and even though I was upstairs, I could smell that mom was cooking bacon. It was like I didn't know I was going to sleep until almost ten, but she knew just when I'd be waking up. It was eerie how she sometimes seemed to know me better than I knew myself, but that's what moms are for, right?

Anyway, I just stayed there like that for a minute. I was in my own bed, the sun was filling up the room, and the smell of bacon was creeping up the stairs. It's the kind of thing you don't notice so much until it's taken away, but I soaked it all in right then. It's like, not to be all mystical or anything, but it's like somewhere deep down I knew what was coming.

I looked out the window to gauge the temperature. It looked warm and I got dressed for that. I pounded down the stairs and headed for the bathroom to brush the morning out of my mouth.

"Morning," Mom called as I passed the kitchen.

"Morning," I said.

"Guess what I'm making," she said. She wanted me to say it, but I refused. It was like my favorite breakfast of all time, English muffins with a slice of melted cheese and a few strips of bacon on top, but she had this real childlike name for it, and I was just too old to be saying stuff like that.

"I'll have four," I yelled back, closing the bathroom door behind me.

I looked in the mirror and my hair was still sticking straight up on the left side from where I'd been sleeping on it, and right then, I thought about Tommy. I didn't know where he was, if he was OK, or what, but standing there in a warm house with my favorite breakfast waiting, looking at my hair sticking up and my face still red from sleep, I hoped he was OK, I hoped he wasn't dead or cold or lost. Then I brushed my teeth, because really, what could I do about it? No need to shower, since it was the weekend.

When I got out, I saw there was already a plate at the table, so I pulled up a chair.

"There you are, four Mommy Surprises for the young gentleman," she said, and I really wished she wouldn't say things like that, but I just thanked her again for the food, and she went back into the kitchen to drain the grease into a Tupperware container. She used it for cooking with. It made everything taste good.

It was just my mom and me, almost since I could remember. I was embarrassed about that for a long time. This was a real small town, so everyone knew your business, and most of the kids around here were a lot better off. Full families, bigger cars, vacations out of town, stuff like that.

It hadn't seemed so bad for a while now. First with Bones and then with Tommy, as messed up as things were for them, I'd gotten to feeling almost lucky. I mean, we had this little house, no one hit me, I got to eat bacon on the weekends. Whatever, I'm not going to tear up here or anything, but I knew it could've been worse.

After breakfast, Mom was like, "What are you going to do today?"

"Well, first off, I'm going out back to dig up some night crawlers," I said. There's a patch out back by the fence where the grass never took that's good for that.

"You going fishing?" she asked.

"Yep," I said. "Mixer, Bones, and me are going up the mountain tomorrow."

Normally, Tommy'd come on a trip like that. There'd be four of us, instead of three. I'm pretty sure we were both thinking it, but neither of us said so. It was just one of those things you didn't say, like how I didn't tell her that Bones didn't really have his license yet. I didn't say he did, either, just let her assume. I never liked to lie to my mom, and so the less I said about this trip the better.

Then she was like, "Well, go change then, if you're going to be digging."

And that is why you really shouldn't have a hard-and-fast policy of not lying to your mom. I should've just said I was going to walk down to the pharmacy. But I went and changed like she said.

As I was walking away, she was still calling after me: "Wear something that's already dirty. Go get those other jeans out of the laundry, the ones you shouldn't still be wearing anyway!"

And then I was outside and it was a little cooler than I thought it was going to be, based on all the sun. It was what the weatherman on channel four would call "clear but cool" or "crisp." Once I got working, though, I wouldn't need a jacket. I rolled up the sleeves of my flannel and went and fished the spade out of the bucket on the porch.

Out back, I kicked away some of the leaves that I'd raked up against the fence until I had a nice patch of dirt and rock to work with. Then I got down on the ground and got to it. I've always liked digging for night crawlers, and I've dug a lot more than I've ever used for fishing. If you've never done it, it's kind of hard to explain. Part of it is I sort of like the smell of dirt: fresh, dark dirt that you just turned over.

There's a song called "Digging in the Dirt" — it goes like, "This time you've gone too far!" — and even though it's by some old English guy, and it's sort of college music and maybe a little gay around the edges, I still sort of like it. I like it because I like digging in the dirt. A lot of times, I ended up sort of humming it when I was digging.

So anyway, I turned over the first rock and there were some grubs or something on the underside of it. White larva sacks, I guess they could also have been some kind of eggs, so I tossed the rock away. Then I just settled in, breaking the dirt with the spade and taking the first few little scoops out. A lot of times, the worms are right near the surface, and you don't want to cut them in half, so you go slow with the spade.

If you do cut them in half, it's pretty cool. They squirm around and crap dirt out of their bodies, but they don't stay alive long enough to fish with if you do that, so you try to avoid it.

Anyway, a few scoops down and I saw the dirt moving, so I brushed it away with my fingers and, sure enough, there was the head of a big fat one, poking around like a finger in the dark. I cleaned a little more dirt away and then pulled it out. Real slow, one long pull, because if you jerk it, it'll tear apart just like if you cut it. You have to be steady, and I'm pretty good at it.

This thing was damn near six inches long, a real monster. I pulled it clear and held it up in the air, just sort of admiring it. The worm curled up like an upside-down question mark. I dropped it in my bucket and dumped some dirt on top.

When you start off the day like that, you know it's going to be a good morning of digging, and I sort of hoped we really did get a chance to go fishing the next day, fishing for something more than answers.

Of course, there was a lot of time between Saturday morning and Sunday afternoon. Most of the time, that was the choice cut of the week, and you just sort of kicked back and let it roll by. This week, it was less choice-cut steak and more pigs' feet or beef tongue or some other thing you didn't necessarily want to be eating. We'd never done anything like this before. I'd never heard of anyone doing it, not to a teacher, so waiting for it opened up a lot of empty hours for nerves and anticipation and second-guessing. I figured disappointment would fit right in on a list like that, so I got cleaned up and biked down to the town library after lunch. They had computers there, too.

Benschotten Memorial Library was a big stone library, left over from when the town was bigger and all that iron money was still rolling in. The other towns around here had little libraries, like in the basement of the town hall or whatever, but we had this thing that looked like half a castle. It had a big clock on top that gonged every hour. The numbers on it weren't 1, 2, 3, they were I, II, III, so you knew it was old.

The place only had two computers, though, so it wasn't handling the twenty-first century quite as well as it had the nineteenth. Both of the computers had senior citizens hunched over them when I got there, so I signed up for "next available computer station" and started waiting. I flipped through the local paper for a while. I always liked the "Police Blotter" part on the inside of the front page, where they listed the car wrecks and drunk and disorderlies and domestic disturbances. They were all like: "Joe Dumbass, 37, of North Cambria was cited for driving too fast for conditions when the vehicle he was driving exited the roadway on Route 44, near the Schuykill turnoff..."

Basically, that meant he hit a tree in the rain and got a ticket, but I sort of enjoyed how formal they made it sound.

It sort of reminded me of that book, now that I thought about it. Whenever I read that page, I always pictured this old Colonel Sanders–looking dude with a bow tie and one of those curled-up mustaches plunking away at a keyboard.

I flipped through a few more stories and then went and stood behind the old dudes at the computers. I stood close so they'd know I was there, like, Move it along, fellas, time to get back to the Home. Finally, one of them stood up, gathered his little stack of books, put his drugstore reading glasses in this little case, and left. He didn't even look back at me, even though I knew he was kind of pissed. That sort of made me sad, because someday I might be that guy, just looking down and moving on when some young punk is in your space. For all I knew, that guy was real hard when he was young.

Anyway, whatever, it was my computer now. I skipped checking my e-mail for the little messages that said "New message from . . ." and went straight to my profile. I mean, that's what I was there for, right? I looked at my lame page: no picture, no blog entries, no comments, but I scrolled down a little and saw that I had "new messages" and "new friend requests." Hot damn, I was like Mr. Popularity all of a sudden.

My heart started beating faster and I got a little light-headed with excitement. I thought about Jenny #2, and I could picture her eyes looking at me, a little smile on her face. I clicked on my inbox first. There was just one message. I sort of hated the way it always said "new messages" even if there was just one. And it was from frickin' Reedy. He wrote exactly one word: *Dude!*

I clicked over to "friend requests," and that was from him, too. Great. I mean, I had nothing against Reedy, except that he was a smartass who I wanted to pop in the mouth about once a day. And he wasn't Jenny #2. Hell, he wasn't a chick at all. I clicked "accept," and went back to my profile to look at where it said I had four friends. That was a little better than before, when I had three.

I sat there letting my pulse slow down. I hated false alarms. Once I'd calmed down a little, I realized that there was someone behind me. I looked over my shoulder and it was that old dude. He'd gone back up and signed up for "next available computer station," and now he was dogging me. Well, good for you, old dude. I didn't think you had it in you. I ignored him anyway.

I went into "pending requests," and a little picture popped up. It was Jenny #2, sitting sideways on the floor somewhere, with her knees pulled halfway up to her chest. She was smiling and she looked pretty, like I remembered her, but from a different angle. From this one, you could sort of almost kind of see down her shirt. So she'd added a picture to her profile. I clicked on her name and she'd added friends, too. She'd added three friends, two girls and a guy, who I didn't know but hated. She had seven friends now.

I sat there and thought about that. She'd accepted other

people's friend requests, just left mine sitting there and clicked "accept" on the ones that had come in after it. Maybe she'd already clicked "deny" on mine, just to clear away the dead wood, so that she could get busy building up her site. Maybe some of those people had sent her messages like, Hey, add me! Just normal messages that they hadn't sat there writing out on notebook paper and tearing up and starting over. But theirs had worked and mine hadn't. Not yet anyway. Maybe she was still thinking about it. Yeah, and maybe Tommy was surfing in Hawaii. Climbing Mt. Everest with a team of penguins.

I logged out and let the old guy have his computer back.

15

After I left the library, I still had most of the day and all of the night to go. You'd think I would've met up with Mixer and Bones to go over our plans for Sunday one more time. Really talk it out, you know, face-to-face. We really should've. Maybe we wouldn't've gone through with it. But we didn't meet up. We just exchanged quick phone calls later on.

Like I said before, things were different between us with Tommy gone. We were starting to pull apart a little. I mean, obviously Mixer and me weren't talking to Bones that much right now. He was in the doghouse, and I think he knew it. But even Mixer and me weren't talking as much as normal. I think we were all spending a lot of time in our own heads, trying to figure all this out.

Of course, everyone's perspective is going to be a little different, and that probably goes double for me. There's one more thing you should know about me, one other thing to say before things get messy.

I haven't explained it up to this point, because it's not necessarily the first thing I tell people about myself, and I'm definitely not here for a pity party, but it's sort of important. When I was a little kid, my face got all busted up. It's not a bad time to get your face busted up, because it's still moving around anyways, and mine has healed up pretty good.

The left side is a little lopsided around the eye, and my left eye kind of droops sometimes. You notice it most if you look at me straight on, but since that's mostly not how people look at each other, I get a lot of double takes. And, yeah, a lot of times I think people are looking at me. They always say they aren't, but they'd say that either way. When I was younger, especially like fourth and fifth grade, I used to get in a lot of fights about my eye. Some kid would say something, and if there was nothing as bad to say back, I'd just start swinging.

My mom doesn't think I remember how it happened, so she tells me it was an accident, that I was on my trike and got going downhill. I remember, though. I'd found something that I wanted to show my dad. It was a shiny hunk of something that I'd turned up in the dirt. I think it was slag or maybe volcano rock, but probably slag, since I don't think there are any volcanoes around here. Anyway, it was shiny and came to a point and I thought it was cool. I don't know why I wanted to show it to my dad, but I'd made up my mind, and at that age, you know, that's that.

He was out in the garage working. I knew he didn't like to be bothered when he was working, but I just toddled right in there anyway. He told me to go away and I told him to take a look and it just went from there. I guess I started wailing at some point, so he shut me up. I don't kid myself about what happened, but I like to think that maybe he forgot his hand wasn't empty when he did it.

I never saw him again after that, at least not that I remember. And as I got older, I was basically OK with that. I'd been too young to really know him, and anyway, he gave me this screwed-up eye to remember him by. Also, he told me that dragonflies would sew your mouth shut if they flew by when it was open, and I believed that until I was like nine. My mom always said we were better off without him and I believed that, too.

Anyway, the point is that I never thought there was anything all that unusual about it. I got hurt bad, and my dad vanished into thin air. It was like the two of us got hit by lightning that day, but he burned up all the way and me only a little. To me it was like, people got hurt, people disappeared, and that's just the way things were. I think, and I've had some time to turn this over, I think it's part of why I was so ready to believe that Haberman might've killed Tommy, killed him and stuck him in a barrel.

A lot of people wouldn't believe a thing like that, but I was there within a day. Right from the start, I was connecting dots that might not've gone together. And I know it seems like Bones and Mixer were on board, too, but Mixer and I were in the habit of agreeing, and Bones was in the habit of going along. I was the one who said it was flesh and bone in that barrel. I was the one who told them how it could've happened.

Having a messed-up eye, you know, it'll affect how you see things.

16

Sunday. This is where it all went to hell. It was a trip we just shouldn't've made, simple as that. We didn't mean for it to go down like it did, at least Mixer and I didn't. Bones, well, it's tough to say what he was thinking. But he did show up armed, and that's got to tell you something. As for me, I just wanted to get a straight answer, either to find out it was real or to put it to rest.

Maybe I'd better just begin at the beginning. We were in Bones's uncle's truck. It was an old beater his uncle kept out by the barn on his farm, and he wasn't going to miss it on a Sunday afternoon. He'd found religion, big-time, and wouldn't ever tend the fields on a Sunday. That's how he put it, "tend the fields." I think maybe that's in the Bible.

Anyway, it's not like we had a lot of options, ride-wise, and Haberman lived kind of far out in Little River. Bones was driving, because it was his uncle's truck and because he had a learner's permit, so it was practically legal. His mom thought it was good enough, anyway. We'd already found the place — the address is right in the phone book — and we'd cruised by once, real slow, to see if there were any other cars in the driveway. We knew there was no Mrs. Haberman, but we were just checking to see if maybe he had company or something.

There were no cars at all in the driveway, but the garage door was open, and we could just see his little MG in there in the shadows. It was late afternoon, kind of a gray day, and as near as anyone knew, we were all three of us up on the mountain fishing. We stopped at the end of the street, and Bones executed the worst K-turn in the history of driving. Bones was wired and on edge. He was geared up for trouble, maybe even looking forward to it. The truck kicked forward with a groan as he threw it back into drive. But there were only three houses on the whole street, all pretty far apart, so the chances of anyone seeing us, or of another car coming along, were pretty slim.

We came up on his house again, this time from the other direction. As we got close, Bones cut the engine and we coasted into the driveway. Bones handled this turn much better than the last one, and it was a nice paved driveway, so even the old rattletrap truck was fairly quiet. Unless Haberman was looking out the window, there was a halfway decent chance he didn't know we were there. Bones pointed the truck off to the right, and we rolled to a stop halfway on the grass, so we wouldn't be as easy to see from the house. We climbed out of the cab real quiet and just pushed the doors shut behind us.

Mixer took a rag or something out of his jacket pocket and put it over the rear license plate of the truck.

"In case anyone drives by," he said.

I gave him a thumbs-up, because it seemed like a pretty good idea to me. There was no shortage of beat-up old pickup trucks around here, so without a license number, it would be hard to find one in particular.

"Thanks," he said, and he was smiling, but you could see it was kind of a nervous smile. I was feeling the butterflies, too.

Looking back, I've got to say, our plan was not really all that solid. I think we'd sort of talked each other into thinking it made sense, but it started to come apart right from the start. I mean, you pretty much lose the element of surprise when you end up standing on the welcome mat and knocking.

But there I was, knocking like a Girl Scout selling cookies. At the last second, after the first knock, Mixer was like, "We'll hide!" And they dove off to the side and crouched down against the wall, and I was left standing there, knuckles in the air. I'm not sure what the point was, except maybe that Haberman was more likely to open the door up for one dude than for three.

And probably of the three of us, Haberman was most likely to open the door for me. I sort of resented the idea of that, like I was some kind of teacher's pet or salvage project or whatever, but I realized by the third knock that it was more or less true. If any of us was thinking clearly, it was Mixer.

Haberman's face appeared in the glass of the door, pale and confused. His thin hair was sticking out at weird angles, and I knew right then that he'd been napping. My breath caught in my throat but I tried not to show it, tried to keep my face totally blank, like Throckmorton's. But this was the wrong time to be thinking about the sheriff, and I felt my pulse rev.

Haberman's eyes narrowed, sized me up. A few quick excuses raced through my head: I was just driving by and had a question about the book; I'm selling something, door to door: Care to order a magazine? A storm door (you really should have one)? Girl Scout cookies?

The door opened and I heard the shush of air slipping in around the weather stripping. It was dark inside and the smell of cigarettes hit me like a breeze.

17

I don't know why Haberman opened the door for me, but I can say for sure that he shouldn't've. I stood there for half a second, looking into the dark gap. I guess the right word is *hesitating*. Then I heard Mixer and Bones stand up, and then there they were, brushing past me on the right and shouldering their way into the house.

"Hey, Mr. H," said Mixer. "Mind if we come in."

But it wasn't a question and they were already inside. I followed and I could feel Haberman pushing the door forward, not hard enough and not in time. It was just like a little protest that meant nothing, one vote against in the face of three votes for. His face was hidden behind the door frame now, but I could imagine the expression he must've been wearing right then, surprise with maybe a little fear mixed in.

By the time I cleared the door and was inside, his expression had settled back to confused. His head looked like it was floating in the air, not attached to anything, because the light was dim in there and he was wearing something dark.

It was a gray day outside — a cold front had swung down overnight and brought a thick layer of clouds with it — and as near as I could tell, there were no lights on in the house. There was just the weak light coming in through the windows to go by. Still, there were plenty of windows, and no need to close the blinds with so few neighbors and even them so far off, so things came into focus fast enough.

Haberman was wearing a dark blue sweat suit under a long bathrobe. The robe was dark plaid and hanging open, as if he'd just thrown it on to get the door. I figured that was the case, but it's still a funny thing to see your English teacher in a sweat suit, slippers, and a raggedy old robe.

There was a staircase straight in front of me, heading up to a landing with a big picture window. The first thing I really noticed, without even taking in all the little things that made it so, was that this was a nice house. Things were nice in here. And apart from the cigarette reek, things were clean.

I looked around. I could see parts of five rooms, including the hallway and what looked to be a kitchen at the far end of it. Pictures were hanging on the wall in frames. Not Wal-Mart frames but real wooden ones. Things were old but not raggedy old, nice old, antique old. When there was a table, it was polished up and there was something on the top of it, like some candles or a bowl of wooden apples.

The room off to the right was sort of a living room, I guess, because it had a couch and a big leather chair in it. I guess in a house like this you might call it a "parlor." I'd heard of parlors but had never been in one before. Or maybe I had, I don't know. Where's the line between a nice, kept-up living room and a parlor? Anyway, that's where we were headed.

Mixer had gone straight for it. I closed the door behind me hard enough to let Haberman know it wasn't negotiable, and the rest of us just kind of drifted in after Mixer, Haberman in between me and Bones, like an animal being herded. At first I figured Mixer picked this room because of the couch, but then I saw a phone on a little table alongside the leather chair. Mixer was standing in between Haberman and the phone, and that was the right thing to do.

I tried to climb inside Haberman's head, figure out what he might be thinking. He couldn't make a break for it. There were three of us; we were young and he was old. The first thing he'd want to do, if he thought he was in danger, which he was, was to get to a phone. There was probably at least one more in the house, plus a cell, if there was service this far out in Little River, which I wasn't sure of.

In any case, we'd have to keep a close eye on him until we were gone. Sunday afternoon in this corner of the state, there wouldn't be anything else for the cops to do. Throckmorton was probably at home, carving up a Sunday bird, but the Staties'd send a cruiser, be here in no time flat.

"Well, gentlemen," he said, and it was sort of a surprise to hear a voice in this dark, quiet house. "What, uh, what brings you to Stavers Street?"

He sounded pretty calm, pretty normal, the tar rolling around in his throat, because he'd been lying down. But just that little hesitation — what, uh, what — that little double-clutch, it told me he was nervous.

And now it was a question of who was going to do the talking, and I figured I'd better, so I threw a "Well" out there, just to box out the other two. Mixer liked to provoke people, and I remembered where things had left off in the parking lot between Haberman and Bones. If either of them did the talking, things could pick up speed fast, not rolling down a hill as much as rolling off a table. Especially if it was Bones.

I looked over at him because something had just sort of dawned on me. He was wearing the camo hunting jacket that used to be his grandad's. That jacket was always a little too big for him, but this far into spring, cold front or not, it was way too much coat, especially since he had a hoodie underneath. I'd sort of thought he'd worn it to look bigger, tougher, like the puffy clothes in the rap videos. The thing about hunting jackets, though, is that they have big, oversized pockets. Bones was keeping his hand in the right-side pocket, with his elbow bent like a gunfighter in a movie, about to draw. I guess that was when I realized he had something in there.

So anyway, yeah, I figured I'd better do the talking, at least to start off. "Oh, we were just kind of passing through, is all," I said, just sort of getting the ball rolling.

"I see," he said. "We don't, uh, get many passersby out here."

He was calling me on it, and that was fair enough, because he knew what I was shoveling.

"This street," he continued, "it only has one end to it."

NO OUTLET is what the sign said, but the phrase "dead end" just sort of hung in the air, waiting to be said. Haberman might've seen it there, though, because he tacked on a quick question. "How did, uh, how did you boys get here?"

"Bones's got a license," I lied.

"Well, congratulations, Mr. Bonouil," Haberman said, turning toward Bones and forcing a thin smile onto his face. "This must be a heady time for you."

"Yeah," said Bones, "real heady."

And he said "heady" the way you might say some unusual swear, like ass-hat.

"Well, if you'll excuse me, gentlemen, I've left something upstairs. I was sleeping, you see."

"What'd you leave?" I asked.

"Uh," he said. There would be a phone up in his bedroom, and I figured that was what he really wanted.

"Your smokes?" I said, giving him a free pass.

"Uh," he said again.

"This won't take long," I said. "You can light up when we leave."

"I wouldn't mind some smokes," said Bones.

"Shut up," I told him, because I figured it was about time to get down to business. He didn't challenge me on it, because I guess he probably figured the same thing.

"Well, then," said Haberman, realizing he wasn't going anywhere and sort of settling onto his heels. "How can I help you?"

Like I said before, our plan was pretty sketchy, but there were a few key parts. First, we'd keep our eyes open for any obvious clues, like blood or stuff like that. And after that, it was basically a shakedown. Haberman was not a big dude, and the three of us standing there, all clenched fists and attitude, we figured that'd be enough. Maybe one of us "accidentally" shoulders into him, maybe we do some shouting, but just to be clear, the plan wasn't to beat it out of him. The plan was to stand there like we *might* beat it out of him — loud and angry, Jack Malone–style — and it seemed like we were all on the same page going in.

We figured if Haberman had anything to do with Tommy, there wouldn't be any problem with us being there, because he'd be the one up the creek. And if it came out he'd killed him, well, we'd probably throw him that beating after all. The cops wouldn't care: We'd be frickin' heroes. And even if he didn't have anything to do with it, if we could get him to spill about what was in the barrel, and it really was road-kill or something like that, he still wouldn't want to cause any trouble.

It was only if we were flat-out wrong on all counts that we'd have problems. If he wasn't guilty of anything more than boring classes, well, that's why we had to keep him away from the phones and stuff. But even if we got nothing, we figured we'd just file out. It would be like, So long, thanks for your time, like he'd just invited us over for tea. Like in *Dumb & Dumber*: "Maybe she'll invite us in for tea and strumpets." What does he charge us with, trespassing? Not if he opened the door. We'd get in trouble at school — because school is a dictatorship and they don't have to prove anything — but we could handle school trouble, no sweat.

And anyway, we were like, This guy's a freak. What are the odds we won't find some dirt on him? We knew he lived alone and half expected to find the house full of shrunken heads or something. The idea was to get our answers and shake something out of him, something bad. Now was the time to start shaking, so I got right to it.

"All right, well," I said, just to get my voice going at a nice even level, "why don't you start by telling us what was in the barrel."

And this look broke out on his face, like sheer relief. He put his hand to his mouth to cover a quick cough, and when he took it away, he had a little smile there. That was definitely not the effect I was going for.

"The barrel? In class? Is that what this is all about?" he said and looked up at the ceiling as if he was scanning it for holes.

"That's a start," I said, and I put a little bite in my voice, because I wanted him to stop smiling. I know he heard it, because he looked down at me and his eyes sort of narrowed. But he didn't say anything, so I kept going.

"Seemed like an animal or something," I said. I was going to start there and work my way up, but Bones jumped in.

"Or a person," said Bones.

"An animal, a *person* . . ." he said, and he said it like it was completely alien and crazy and he had no idea what we were talking about. The tricky thing about that was that it was exactly how you'd expect him to react if we were wrong and he had nothing to hide, but it was also exactly how you'd expect him to act if we were right and he did.

"Well, gentlemen, I can assure you it was no such thing. I certainly couldn't bring a — what are you saying? — a *carcass* onto school property."

"Yeah, why did you then?" said Bones. He still had his right hand in his jacket pocket, and I saw something shift in there.

This was why Bones shouldn't've been talking, because he was just going to accuse Haberman and Haberman was just going to deny it. Of course he was. I thought it might open up an angle for me, though, allow me to be like the Voice of Reason.

"Well, I'll tell ya," I said, trying to sound sort of neighborly or whatever, "sure felt like something was shifting around in there."

"Well, yes," said Haberman, looking over at me, then right back at Bones, because now he'd noticed Bones's right hand buried in the jacket pocket, too. His eyes drifted back to me as he spoke. "It was, I mean, it was just . . ."

"Well, spit it out," said Bones, and I sort of cringed, because it'd seemed like that's exactly what Haberman was about to do before Bones piped up. And even if it was going to be a lie, it still would've been something to start with and build off. Now, Haberman had zipped it again. He was just standing there and looking at Bones.

I guess Bones had a lot of steam stored up, all that stuff he couldn't say or do in class, because of that F hanging over his head, that threat of having to repeat. It was pretty clear he wasn't going to bottle it up here, I guess because it wasn't the class or even the school. Mixer was looking at Bones with kind of an amazed expression. Mixer knew what was going to happen. I didn't yet, or maybe I did but thought it could still be avoided, so I butted in again.

"What about all that talk?" I said. "About a murder at the school and disposing of a body and who would the police believe?"

I just kind of blurted it all out at once. It wasn't how I'd planned it, but Bones was really kind of speeding things up, the way he was acting. Haberman only glanced over at me toward the end. Mainly, he was keeping his eyes on Bones.

"Well, that, that was just the book. I was talking about the book."

"I don't think so."

"Yeah," said Bones. "See, Mike here, he read your stupid book."

Haberman looked at me now, and I tipped my head and took credit for it, even though I hadn't exactly finished.

"He doesn't dispose of the bodies," I said, hoping there wasn't a scene like that past where I'd read. "Just leaves 'em there."

"You're right," said Haberman, and I think I might've actually blushed. It was dim in the house, though, so I don't think anyone saw. I hope no one did.

"I suppose I was speaking hypothetically."

"That's not what you said before."

"Quite right," he said, and at this point, he was looking at me. "I was creating a scenario that you might be able to relate to more easily. I was just trying to, well, to get your attention."

"Well, you got it."

"I should say."

"Where'd you get an idea like that: a kid killed at school, in a classroom? Problems for his friends?" I said.

"Well, I, uh . . ." he said.

"What was in the damn barrel?" shouted Bones, interrupting.

Haberman jumped and I think I did, too.

Haberman turned toward Bones with his head sort of pulled in toward his shoulders, like he was expecting to be hit. At this point, I was pretty much the only one who didn't know.

"It was just . . ." he said.

"Yeah?" said Bones.

"Some trash," said Haberman, and that really set Bones off.

"Oh, that's it," he said. "That is frickin' it."

And Bones stepped forward. His right hand came out of his jacket, and he was holding that stupid fish club. I knew where he'd gotten it. I'd considered taking it myself. Right then, a few things dawned on me. It's funny how violence coming on can make you think clearer.

The first thing I realized was that when Haberman said trash, that's exactly what he meant. I tested it out in my head: a week's worth of trash, not the wet stuff, but the recyclables and the big stuff. People around here, they saved it up and made a run to the transfer station every few weeks. It would be like some old newspapers, a broken-up chair, a busted blender, that kind of stuff. Yeah, I thought, that could move like that. Those knobs pushing out against the blanket, they could've come from one thing with limbs or from loose pieces, like two-by-fours, wrapped up together. Not sure why it'd be so heavy, but then, how did I know what he was throwing out?

The other half of that was that when Haberman said trash, Bones thought he was talking about Tommy. It was a dangerous misunderstanding, because there wasn't much Haberman could do now. Bones was just a few feet away, stronger and faster and the one holding the club.

"Recognize this?" said Bones.

"Where? How did you get that?" said Haberman.

"In your desk drawer," said Bones. "You really should get a better lock for that. You've got a bad element in your class."

That last part was a threat. He was mocking Haberman, trying to provoke him. The whole thing about the club was a threat. I mean, it was just a little piece of wood, maybe eight or ten inches long. Bones could do just about as much damage with his hands and more with his boots, but it was a weapon, and holding it out there in the open like that, well, it pretty much told you what you needed to know. You hold up a leash, the dog goes bonkers because he knows he's going for a walk. You hold up a cigarette, it means you're going to smoke. You hold up a club . . .

I guess Haberman had figured out that reasoning with Bones wasn't going to do much good at this point, because he wheeled around and looked at me. He either wanted me to help, to call off the dog, or he was relying on Bones not to hit an unarmed man in the back. As it turned out, he had the wrong man in both cases.

Haberman was looking at me, the back of his head just wide open for the club, and I was looking past him at Bones. Bones looked back and gave a quick little wink, and so then I thought, All right, he's just bluffing, raising the stakes, and I had to give it to him, because I figured Haberman would tell us just about anything at this point.

"It was just, let's see, some boards and most of a bucket of plaster and . . ." He kept talking but I latched on to the plaster, heavy and still a little wet in its jumbo-sized plastic bucket, a soft center, left over from some fixer-upper project. They'll sell that stuff as a powder, but it gets real heavy when you mix the water in. We dump all that stuff in the trunk, he drives it straight over to the transfer station, maybe half a mile from the school.

"You think —" he went on, his voice shaking. "You think it was your friend, Mr. Dawson, the one who's been absent all week? You think I killed him and put him in that barrel?"

Haberman had either finally put it together or he was finally ready to admit it.

"But that's," he said, and he took a half step, "that's crazy!"

He looked at me and then over at Mixer. His shoulders were tensed up in case some wood was about to fall between them, and the way he said *crazy*, I was just like, Oh, crap. Because he meant it. I could tell he meant it. He taught English, not drama. There was no way he was that good of an actor. And then he knocked down a few more of our lame clues at once, like picking up a split in bowling.

"The trash was for the transfer station and the barrel was from out behind the school; it's been there all year," he said. "It was Hank's" — I put on my dumb face, not knowing who Hank was, and he backtracked — "It was Grayson's idea to use it. He told me your class — how did he put it? — 'responded' to that sort of thing."

I was thinking a few things here. First: Yeah, that's where I'd seen that barrel before. Second: It seemed like something Mr. G would do; even at the time I'd thought that. I'd seen those two talking before, had seen them coming out of the teachers' lounge. They still seemed kind of mismatched to me, like a dog hanging out with an alligator, but what did I know? They were both teachers, about the same age, both kind of weird, when you got right down to it. Haberman really didn't need to keep talking at this point. The defense could pretty well've rested, but I guess he still had one more half-assed theory to shoot down.

"Where did I get the idea, a student killed in between classes?" he said, and he was sort of pleading now. "*Law & Order!*"

Law & Order... Damn... I'd been watching the wrong show.

18

Haberman was standing right in the middle of the room, and that's where Bones attacked him with the club. It surprised the hell out of me, because at that point, my brain was working a mile a minute to come up with some kind of exit strategy. Maybe tell him something like, Sorry for your time, you've got a real nice house here, and then a quick retreat. But that's not how it happened. I guess Haberman saw my eyes go wide as Bones raised the club, because he swung around just in time to catch the first shot on his right forearm. He'd raised it to defend himself, but it didn't matter. The club made a dull thud that ended with a crack I could hear three feet away. Bones had broken Haberman's arm with the first swing.

From there, Bones just went to work. It was a bad scene. Haberman was clutching onto Bones's left side with his busted arm, and Bones just kept rearing back with his right and letting him have it.

I was surprised that Haberman didn't scream, but I guess he was always more of a talker. He blurted out words in bursts. He said, "Please stop" and stuff like that. He talked fast and desperate but not loud until right before the end.

I stutter-stepped toward him, toward Bones, toward both of them, but not really. I don't know if you watch basketball, but I watch the Celtics sometimes. In basketball terms, I stutter-stepped and gave maybe a little shoulder fake, but it wasn't a fake, because I really meant to go. I'd sent the get-going signals to my body; I just wasn't following them up with the keep-going ones. Something was holding me back, loyalty, I guess, and probably some fear. There was blood now, and that club flying around. Whatever it was, it all added up to a half step with my left foot and a turn of my left shoulder, like I was leading with it, like I was really going to go. Bones wasn't biting on the fake. He wasn't even looking.

I wanted him to stop, I swear to god I did, but wanting wasn't going to get it done. In order for that to happen, I was going to have to get in there, push him away, maybe tackle him, maybe fight. And that was a big step. Picking the guy who'd been my teacher for seven months over the one who'd been my friend for almost seven years? And fighting about it? That was going to take some working up to, some serious rewiring of my brain.

I was pretty sure Mixer was pulling out the circuits in his

head, too. I looked over at him. He was staring at the action. His mouth was open and his hands were out to either side, like in dodgeball, when someone's lining you up and you don't know which way you're going to have to jump. I couldn't exactly tell what he was thinking, but I was pretty sure that if I went over there, he'd go, too.

It was like part of me wanted to do it — to take Bones to the ground and hold him there until he got a grip or at least until Mixer got there to help — and another part of me just wasn't ready for that. And it's not like that second part won; it just held out for long enough. It was all over pretty quickly. All I did was shout at him a few times — "Bones!" I'd said. "Bones!" — and he could read whatever he wanted into that. Hell, maybe he thought I was cheering for him.

Maybe six or seven shots in, Bones brought the club down flush on the top of Haberman's head. It made a sound like kicking a rotten log, and Haberman fell onto his side. It was hard to tell if he was knocked out or worse. He curled up like a baby, with his face toward me. His eyes were closed, and I could see that there was an angry slash of deep red on the bridge of his busted nose.

For a second or two, everything was quiet. Bones just stood there, looking down, and I could see that he had a long red stripe cutting down from his neck to his chest and a few little dots on his face. It looked like he'd been slashed, but I knew it wasn't his blood. That nose must've just exploded.

"Holy . . ." I said.

"Jesus," said Mixer.

"He didn't do it," said Bones.

Bones knew, just like I did. He knew Haberman hadn't done anything, and he attacked him anyway — I think he may've been trying to kill him. And you know what I was thinking right then? I was thinking I should've known. I should've known this would happen or at least that it could've. Bones'd nearly gone after Haberman right outside the school doors, in the parking lot. What'd I think he'd do a full town over?

But I didn't think about what would happen, just about what could happen, how it could all work out if everything went perfect. And that was my fault, because when was the last time that things went perfect for me or even well? And Bones nodding his head and saying, "Yeah, sure," when we were planning things, well, that obviously didn't mean jack. I don't know if he had his own plan the whole time or if he just didn't have ours. It amounted to the same thing.

And now Bones had a little smile on his face. I remembered him talking about Haberman in the cafeteria and saying "I hate that guy," just like he'd said "I hate that kid" after he'd beaten Adam down outside the pizza place. And here's what I thought right then and what I still think. When Bones saw Haberman standing there, he saw every F that'd ever landed face-up on his desk and every smirking teacher who'd ever put it there. Then he saw Haberman wriggling off the hook, shooting down our stupid theories, and he knew if he hadn't done it right then, he never would've gotten another chance.

19

There's no use crying over spilled milk, and it's not like I was going to cry, just like it wasn't milk spilling out of Haberman's shattered nose. But I was kind of riled up, just the same. I'd felt frozen and torn while it was happening, but my feet had come unstuck now. Bones had screwed everything up, and he was smiling about it. I had a powerful urge to run up and tackle him, just take him to the floor and pound him, Ultimate Fighter–style.

"What the hell?" I said. "You crazy son of a bitch! What are we supposed to do now? Could we be more screwed?"

I was just rattling it off, but even then, I had to hold back. Bones still had the club in his hand. He still had blood down his front and a little bit of maniac in his eyes.

Mixer started in on him, along the same lines as what I was saying, but I reached over without looking and tapped him on the arm. He got the message and zipped it. We just had to let the adrenaline drain out of Bones for a bit.

When it did, I stepped forward and bent down over Haberman. I put my hand against his neck, like I'd seen on TV. I knew I was looking for a pulse, but I didn't know where exactly to find it. I pressed down with all four fingertips in order to cover more territory. Finally, I found something. It was weak but it was there.

"He's alive," I said. "I guess we should leave him on his side like this."

"Yeah," said Mixer. "In case he pukes."

I stood up and took a step back toward Mixer. It felt like in gym class, when you pick teams.

"Well," said Bones, "I guess we got our answers."

"Yeah," said Mixer, "so what the hell was the beat-down for?"

"Had to see if he was telling the truth, right?"

"That doesn't make one damn bit of sense."

"Yeah, well, it worked well enough. And we needed to send him a message anyway. We got nothing on him. He didn't do nothing, and that means we shouldn't be here."

"Yeah, you're right," said Mixer. "You're absolutely right. I sure wouldn't want to get, what, detention? What did we really do? What did we really do — until you beat the crap out of him? You want trouble, what do you think is going to happen once he wakes up?"

"If he wakes up," said Bones.

I was going to say something like, No, I just checked on him. He'll be OK. Then I realized what Bones was saying.

"No way, man," I said. "I don't need that kind of trouble. We're screwed now, but that's a whole 'nother level of screwed."

"At what point did you become such a freakin' psycho?" said Mixer. "You're not doing anything else, not so much as breathe on him."

And I guess I saw it move, because I looked down at the club. There was a little blotch of blood on the side, and right then, Bones tightened his grip on it. Maybe it'd been slipping, but it seemed like he did it because Mixer was telling him what he could and couldn't do. I looked up at him, and it was like, Just try it, if you think you can club your way through the both of us. We're not middle-aged English teachers, not talk-first types. I said before that I didn't think I could match his intensity most of the time, his mean streak. This was one of the times I thought I could. I could, and I was pretty sure Mixer could, that we could tear him apart, that we'd enjoy it.

It was quiet for a second. Mixer had his hand in his pocket, and I knew he was fishing around for that little orange-handled knife of his. It'd be a pretty lame arms race: fish club vs. tiny knife, but it didn't come to that. Bones loosened his grip and let his shoulders drop.

"Well," he said, "what's your big plan then? You two want to go get him an aspirin and a Band-Aid or something?"

I didn't appreciate the sarcasm but I let it go. I looked down: Haberman hadn't moved at all since I found that weak pulse.

"Man," I said. "I don't know."

"We got to wait on him," said Mixer, "wait till he comes to."

"Yeah, and what are we going to do then?" said Bones.

"We got to let him know that there's more where that came from. Got to make him swear not to talk. Say we'll come back, unless he says he fell down the stairs or something."

"Yeah, great," I said, "except he could just call the cops and get us locked up, and unless he happens to wander within two feet of our jail cell, there's not much we'd be able to do to him."

"Nuh-uh," said Bones. "We've got rights."

It was probably the dumbest thing I'd ever heard anyone say, and I just looked at him.

"Well, I don't know," said Bones. "We can say he was abusing us or something. Like he invited us over here to mess with us."

"Yeah, and who are they going to believe?" I said, and there was that phrase again.

"We don't really have to say that," said Mixer, testing it out, "just tell him we're going to say that he was molesting us. Stuff like that goes straight to the news, and he won't want the trouble. And there'll be a trial and all that. I don't think most teachers get beaten by their students. It will, I don't know, look bad."

"I don't know," I said, but it was Mixer talking now, so I was willing to listen.

"Yeah, we'll say all that, then tell him all he has to do is say he fell down that big flight of stairs. No rumors, no trial, no second beat-down, and we'll be like model students until we die or graduate."

"Yeah," said Bones. "That could work."

"Worth a shot," Mixer said.

"Well, I guess we can wait a while," I said. "It's not like he didn't already see us."

I looked down, still no movement, but the bleeding had stopped.

"I got to say, though, it could be a long wait."

"We got time," said Bones. "The fish ain't biting."

And that was it, it's like the decision had been made. It was the wrong decision. I already knew that. What I should've done was get to a phone, make some excuse to shake Bones, and then dial 911. I needed to get an ambulance here. But I felt guilty, involved, just for being there, for not stopping him. And we still didn't know how bad it was. They record those calls, and I didn't want my voice sitting there, waiting to get matched up in some police lab. You see that on TV all the time, they play back the audio, and the voices become these squiggly lines on a monitor, and when those lines match up, someone goes to jail.

Bones should be the one to call, but I knew he wouldn't. He'd frickin' laugh at the idea. Instead, he walked over toward the couch.

"Don't!" I shouted, and the three of us stood there and waited.

Odds were, it wasn't going to matter if we left prints or fibers or any of that other CSI stuff. As soon as Haberman came to, there'd be a witness wearing all the evidence he needed on his face. It would only matter if he didn't remember what happened. Considering the shots he'd taken to the head, I wasn't ready to rule that out just yet. Of course, if that was our out, we shouldn't have still been standing there. The other possibility was that he wouldn't come to at all. Beatings like that, they were for the young. That's why the couch was off-limits, because it would really matter then. We all knew the stakes. We were waiting around for him to wake up or for him not to.

We didn't talk much.

"Anyone have a watch?"

"There's a clock over in the hall."

And then another few minutes of silence.

"Should we do something?"

"Like what?"

"I don't know, get him one of those little pillows over there?"

"Nah."

More silence.

"Well," I said after a while, "I guess we got one answer. We know Haberman didn't have anything to do with Tommy. Dammit, Tommy. He really should give us a heads-up before he pulls this stuff. But we know that. You guys heard him. He was totally clueless, didn't know jack. And, man, once that club came out, he would've told us anything. So we got one answer."

"And we know what was in the barrel," said Bones, like this was a test and we were getting points per question.

"Who the hell cares what was in the barrel?" I said.

"That was the whole point!" said Bones.

And now *that* was the dumbest thing I'd ever heard. He was just breaking records left and right.

An hour later, Haberman still hadn't moved, and it was getting uncomfortable to stand. I bent down to check his pulse again, to make sure, and also to bend my knees a little. The pulse was still there but still weak. I was starting to think he was more than just knocked out. I put my hand in front of his mouth. Same thing there: not much.

"I got to take a leak," said Mixer.

"Not here," I said.

Mixer gave me a quick little look, not mean, exactly, but sharp. And it was true: No one had elected me leader.

"Well," he said, "I got to tell you, pretty soon, it's going to be here. One way or the other."

"Yeah," I said. "We can't stay here much longer, anyway."

"Yeah," said Bones. "I think he got the point, anyhow."

I looked at him, hoping that maybe he was right. I was like a poker player, counting my outs. As near as I could tell, I had three: memory loss, intimidation, or death. I was pulling for the first option.

"I've got to do something about this," said Bones, motioning down his front. "Need some water or something."

"Maybe the kitchen," I said. "But wipe down anything you touch."

And that was that. There was nothing left to do except walk out on stiff legs and open the door with the sleeve of my shirt. That, and wonder if this guy was going to make it. If he didn't, I figured the law wouldn't much care who'd done the beating and who'd done the watching and waiting.

We left him there on the floor, half on his nice rug, half off. Outside, it was almost dark. The first stars might've been out, but it was too cloudy to see them. We climbed back in the truck and backed out onto the road. No one coming from either direction, just some house lights on farther up the street, and we were gone.

"You better drive like a frickin' grandmother," I told Bones.

"No problem," he said, but he was already going too fast.

Back at the house, Bones had wiped himself off with a kitchen towel. He'd cleaned off his face and what he could of his front. Then he'd wiped down the club and stuffed it in his jacket pocket with the wet towel. It was good enough: dark-blue sweatshirt, camo jacket. What was left of the stain barely showed.

Now he had the heat turned all the way up to dry off, and Mixer and me were cooking in our own sweat. It felt like we were driving straight into hell, and none of us talked much as Bones made the circuit, dropping me off first. We were all lost in our own thoughts, I guess, playing out scenarios in our heads.

"I guess we just wait now," Bones said as I pushed the door open to get out.

"I guess," I said.

"Don't say anything," he said. "Just the same."

Just the same meant in case Haberman died. It wouldn't much matter what I said otherwise.

"Yeah," I said. "Sure."

Mixer'd been stuck in the middle, and he slid over as I got out. He was facing me and mouthed something that wasn't meant for Bones to catch. I was pretty sure the first two words were "We are." The last word began with an f, because he put his lower lip under his front teeth like you do when you make an f. I slammed the door on the rest, but I figured I got the message.

Turned out, I was wrong about what he was saying, but my way would've worked, too. A bad plan had broken down into almost no plan at all. I expected to get the third degree when I got inside, but there were too many thoughts flying around in my head, and it was just like a buzz. I couldn't focus at all. My mom was standing in the kitchen when I opened the door.

"Catch anything?" she said.

"What?" I said.

I'd left my fishing gear in the back of the truck, the pole and gear, the little container of night crawlers.

20

It took me forever to get to sleep that night. That's not all that unusual for me, but that night, in particular, it was like, Why bother? It really seemed like they could come for me anytime, banging on the door in the middle of the night, just like in the movies. I just stayed there under the covers, over-heated and stewing in my own juices, turning it over in my head a thousand times.

Here's the thing, straight up: I'd done nothing. Nothing useful, anyway. That was good and that was bad. I mean, if someone was going to call me on it, I'd say, "What? I didn't do anything!" And if someone was going to accuse me, they'd be like, "He didn't do anything."

And both sides would be right. I hadn't so much as touched Haberman. Well, I had, but that was just to check his pulse. Also, and I think you could argue this part forever, but I'm pretty sure I stopped Bones from going back in for round two.

On the other hand, I hadn't done anything to stop him during round one. I mean, not jumping in on a beating you could sort of see. A guy could get hurt that way. I'd yelled out, but I'd yelled the wrong thing. I should've yelled "Stop," to get myself on the record as being against what was happening, instead of "Bones," which only got me on the record as knowing his frickin' nickname. I mean, at least I could've said something useful like "not on the head," but I didn't even do that.

Mixer didn't do anything, either. I'm not pointing fingers, but for a second I thought maybe I could claim peer pressure's what turned me into such a lump. At the school, they were always talking about "the adverse effects of peer pressure" and stuff like that. But I realized pretty quick that peer pressure is not a topic you ought to be raising when it was your idea to go there in the first place. I mean, what was I supposed to say, "But, Your Honor, it was just supposed to be a shakedown."

It's like, damned if you do, damned if you don't. The fact remained that I'd done nothing, and it all sort of branched out from there. I thought of him lying there on the floor, his cheek streaked with nose blood and me working hard to find a pulse. What if he died?

If he bought it after I stood around watching, I'd be charged with that, with letting it happen. I thought about it, and the mistakes we made hit me one at a time. It was like a line of people waiting their turn to hit me in the gut with a baseball bat. There'd be tire tracks in the yard from where Bones'd pulled off to the side so the truck would be tougher to spot. Tracks from tires so old the police'd know they came from a truck that didn't see much road. That'd mean a truck kept in a garage or a barn.

And my frickin' fishing gear was in that truck, those night crawlers dying in there slow.

And there'd be footprints. There'd be two pairs of tracks from where Mixer and Bones waited in the soft dirt along the house. And inside, I'd wiped down everything we touched — at least I think I did — but it's not like I wiped my feet on that stupid mat before I went in. And I'd touched him, checked for a pulse. I didn't think they could get prints off a man's neck, but I didn't know for sure.

And all this applied if he lived and had the memory of what happened knocked out of his head. All of it except maybe the fingerprints-on-the-neck thing. But that was stupid anyway: Amnesia was for the movies. Relying on it in real life was like relying on magic elves or something.

But if he didn't die, and he didn't forget, well, then what was taking him so long? I looked over at my alarm clock. He'd be at the hospital by now, all cleaned up and asleep in his little white bed. He would've already told them everything he knew: the who, what, why, and they'd already know the where. He probably would've said what'd happened to him when he called for the ambulance. Dialing 911 was really one-stop shopping when it came to stuff like that.

Back at the house we'd thought maybe he wouldn't tell because he'd be afraid of us, but really, fear was a better reason to tell the cops than not to. And so it was back to waiting for that knock on the door, wondering if I'd even have time to get dressed before they hauled me off. Wondering what my mom would think, would she even be surprised?

I must've dozed off for a bit, because I woke up with a start at around four. There was a thought in my head, and it was so clear and up-front that it was like the thought is what woke me up, like it just wouldn't let me ignore it anymore. I guess it was two thoughts really, but they were all tangled together. One: I should call the cops, just tell them what happened, how I hadn't meant it, how it was all Bones. Because, two: Friendships end. It happens every day.

It seemed so obvious, but I knew better. I'd had all kinds of crazy thoughts in the middle of the night, lying there bleary-eyed and fuzzy-minded. I once had myself half convinced that I could move the alarm clock with my mind. So I tried to calm down and untangle it all, just to see if it really made sense. After a few minutes, I knew that it might've, but that it definitely wasn't as clear-cut as it'd seemed when I woke up.

Yeah, friendships ended, but there was a fine line between moving on and cutting out when things got tough. Ditching

a friend . . . it just sounded bad. It seemed like the guy walking away was always the dick. And even a dick with a good
excuse is still a dick. I'd always thought I could trust Bones
before, and now I wasn't sure. But I was the one thinking
about turning him in, so really, who couldn't trust who?

The sleep was coming back and it was hard to focus my
thoughts. I tried again. It's like they say, your girlfriend cheats
on you with your best friend, dump the girl. Of course, that's
a pretty easy thing to say when you don't have a girlfriend.
And Bones wasn't my best friend, either. But the general idea
still seemed to apply: You can let a lot go, if a guy's your
friend. It's supposed to mean something.

Bones hadn't stuck to the plan and he'd screwed us over,
but it wasn't all that different from the stuff he'd been pulling
for years. Yeah, it was more serious, and it was a teacher this
time. But I hadn't walked away before, and it's not like I
hadn't had plenty of warning.

As for calling the cops, well, it seemed like I'd missed that
boat. It wasn't so much that I should do it now as that I
should've done it then. If I'd done it right away, if I'd snuck
upstairs to Haberman's room and hit 911, for the cops and
the ambulance, too, then maybe we could've sold Bones up
the river, made it a solo trip for him. But then I was right
back to the thing about sticking by your friends, and that
branched off into the friendships end thing. I remembered
Throckmorton sitting across from me, his face impossible to
read. I just didn't know, and it didn't matter anyway, because

what did I do instead of dialing 911? I wiped our prints off the furniture and stood there watching the guy bleed.

But maybe it wasn't too late. I tried to pull it all apart and piece it back together, but I was so tired. Words floated into my head, just pieces of a sentence: "with painful concentration he looked around . . . the floor . . . everywhere . . . trying to make sure he hadn't forgotten anything. . . ." At first I couldn't remember where I'd heard it, but then I remembered. I hadn't heard those words at all. I'd read them.

The night was quiet outside, just the spring sounds of insects and wind. I looked over at my alarm clock, and I knew the light would be creeping into the room soon, and not long after that, I'd have to get up and go to school. I couldn't afford not to go, just in case. It'd be Monday morning, and we'd have Yanoff for English. That's how it would all start. The alarm clock would have to tell me when. I fell back asleep.

21

Mixer wasn't on the bus, and I was thinking, Man, I hope he isn't ditching. That'd really look suspicious. A few stops later, Natalie got on the bus. It was the first time I'd seen her since the house in the woods. I sunk down in my seat as she walked by. I was surprised I could feel worse about myself than I already did. I thought for sure I'd bottomed out. She didn't look at me, but then she never did. Well, almost never.

Without Mixer there, I had a long bus ride by myself to think about things. Maybe he figured we were going to get hauled off today anyway, and decided to get hauled off from home instead of getting dragged out of class by the cops. That wasn't a bad call, and I wondered if the driver'd let me off at the next stop, like if I said I'd forgotten something or had to puke. Probably not, I decided, and a move like that would be a whole new level of suspicious.

I rode it out, and it turned out Mixer was in school, anyway. His dad'd given him a lift. We met up at our lockers but didn't say much more than "hey" to each other. I always felt sort of underwater after not sleeping much; everything was slower, and that included my mouth. He looked bad and I probably looked worse. It felt like I was behind enemy lines and under fire. Just turning corners in the hallway seemed dangerous. Seeing Mixer felt like that scene in the war movies, where the guy jumps into a foxhole and his buddy's already in there, reloading.

We passed Bones on the way to homeroom — his homeroom was at the other end of the same hallway. He looked like death, and that seemed kind of appropriate. With him, it wasn't like seeing a war buddy, but it wasn't like seeing an enemy, either. We all held our fire. We talked a little but broke it off after ten or fifteen seconds. The stuff we had to talk about had to be whispered, and at that point, it seemed pretty dumb for the three of us to be out in the open, huddled together and whispering. I just told him I needed my fishing gear back, and he just told me he'd get it. I said tonight, and he said no problem.

After the door closed on homeroom and the final bell went off, I sat at my desk thinking, Is this where it's going to happen? Is that door going to be opened by the kind of men who don't care much about hall passes or final bells, Throckmorton with that big gun on his hip or Staties in their dark *Empire Strikes Back*–looking uniforms?

The door opened, but it was just Max. He was late and rattling off excuses. That just seemed pathetic to me, arguing over that kind of trouble. Take your frickin' demerits and sit down, jackass. Some of us have real problems and don't want to hear it. The bell rang and released us. Monday schedule, first-period Spanish, which was just like insult to injury. Mixer and I went our separate ways where the hall turned off at the library. I looked out the front windows for cruisers. There weren't any, but that wasn't much comfort, because I knew those things swooped in fast.

I was stupider than usual in Spanish. Ms. Chaney was saying the phrases as she wrote them on the board, and it just sounded like nonsense syllables, like a big baby babbling. About the only words I caught were *el* and *la*. Fifteen minutes to go, first period, and the phone on Chaney's desk started ringing. Aw, Christ, I thought. *Hasta la vista*, everyone.

Chaney put down her chalk and walked over to her phone. It was one of those big, blocky phones that no one has at home anymore. On TV, they are always red and patched straight through to the White House or the Bat Cave or some-place like that. In real life, they are tan and sit in between stacks of paper on teachers' desks or in hospitals maybe.

She picked up the phone and listened to a short message without changing her expression. I had already closed my note-book and begun stacking my books when she called my name. "Miguelito, they'd like to see you in *la oficina*," she said, mixing in enough English so that she wouldn't have to repeat herself.

My heart didn't skip a beat and the world didn't stop spinning. It felt like I was rolling down an assembly line, like this was the next stop. If I was an action figure, this would be where the lady put my arms on. The next stop, they'd remove my head. I didn't want to hold things up, so I picked up my stuff and headed toward the door.

"*Si*, Señora Chaney," I said.

The hall was empty. There was no one waiting to meet me, and if they were going to slap the cuffs on me, they were going to do it in *la oficina*. That kind of pissed me off. They just expected me to walk myself into custody. But it was true, and they must've known that. I didn't have many other options: no car, no place to go. I had no real desire to run off and live on a heating grate on the street somewhere, not to avoid my share of an assault rap, anyhow. And if it was more than that, they definitely would've come for me. I didn't want to be a killer — or even a part-killer — so in a way, I was kind of relieved. But mainly it just sucked. Jail or juvie: I'd heard there wasn't much difference. Either way, it'd be bad.

I started walking. I was going slow, because I figured the least I could do was make them wait. I looked out the second-floor windows as I went. I had a good view of the front parking lot from there, but I couldn't make out any cruisers or sheriff's department cars. I figured maybe they'd parked out back.

I guess this makes me a juvenile delinquent, I was thinking as I started down the north stairwell. A lot of people considered me one anyway, but I figured this'd make it official. Mixer and Bones were waiting for me at the bottom of the stairs. They knew I'd come this way. They'd come from shop, and Mixer still had red lines around his eyes from the safety goggles.

"Two more steps if you're screwed," he said.

I took the last two steps and I was.

"Hey," said Bones, once I was next to them. "We've got to square up what we're going to say."

That seemed like a good idea.

"I've been thinking about that," he said, and his voice was a strong, hissy whisper.

That made one of us. In all the time I'd spent beating this thing to death in my head — probably a bad choice of words there — I hadn't once thought about what to do if it came down to this. Down to us telling our version of the story. I'd just sort of assumed that they'd either come for us or they wouldn't, and if they did, they'd just sort of decide what to do with us. I'd just fast-forwarded to the jailhouse door slamming shut in front of me.

But of course there was more to it than that: statements, maybe a trial, that kind of stuff. We had to soften it up some, make Haberman look worse and us look better. We should've gotten right to it. Instead, Bones and Mixer started arguing.

"Yeah, I'll bet you have," said Mixer.

"What d'you mean by that, Malloy?"

"Nothing. As long as your plan doesn't include saying that anyone other than you swung that club."

"Shut the hell up!" said Bones. "Don't say club."

"Like they won't be able to figure that out."

"It's the difference between assault and assault with a deadly weapon."

"That thing's only deadly if you're a fish," I said.

I was hoping more than saying, but I was trying to get between them and get us talking about what we needed to be talking about. This all sounded a little familiar, all this back and forth, and I realized that this was in that book, too. The dude keeps running over the same territory from different directions. What if I do this? What if I don't? What if they think this? What if they think that?

Of course, in the book, there's just the one guy keeping the secret. But there were three of us here now. In a way that was better, because we weren't alone with it. We could talk it out and plan. But in another way, it was worse, because it was three times the mouths to keep shut. I mean, the Russian dude had to sort of argue with himself, but we could argue with each other. And it's just simple math. More people knew, and if enough people know something, it's not really a secret anymore.

One guy or three, it all amounted to the same thing: freaking out about getting caught. I mean, the title of the book is *Crime and Punishment*, and that could end up working for us, too. Right now, we were hovering somewhere over the "and." If we didn't want to take that next step, we needed to get our story straight.

"No, seriously," Bones was saying. "I looked it up."

"What," said Mixer, "on the Internet?"

"Yeah."

"You dumbass, they can trace that."

"What?"

And that was as far as we'd gotten — debating whether or not to mention a club that Haberman and any decent doctor in the world would know we used — when Trever walked by the stairwell.

"There you three are," he said, stopping and turning toward us.

Mixer's eyes got huge and Bones's knees bent down, as if he was going to make a break for it. I went light-headed but stayed on my feet. Trever took it all in but didn't respond. I guess he was used to scaring kids.

"They want to see you three in the office," he said. He was wearing a blue suit with white stripes that you'd miss if you didn't look close. He looked like a politician. The office was back in the direction he'd been coming from. I wondered if they'd sent him out to round us up. Strange that the cops would send the assistant principal out to bring us back. Maybe they did it because he knew what we looked like and where shop and Spanish were. Or maybe they hadn't sent him.

He went on: "I might as well spare you the trip, though."

"What's up, Mr. Trever?" said Mixer. I was glad he spoke up, because I didn't trust my voice right then.

"Archie just wanted to let you know" — Archie was Principal Throckmarten — "that they found your friend."

"Where did they find him?" I said after a few long seconds. The way he said "found him," I thought maybe he meant his body, and maybe I was right after all.

"The McDonald's," said Trever.

"In North Cambria?" said Bones.

"That's the one," said Trever.

I knew there were no shallow graves at the McDonald's and that Tommy was fine. I wasn't all that surprised. As soon as we knew that Haberman hadn't done anything to him, I knew Tommy was liable to come waltzing back, no warning, just like he left. But the timing on this one was a real kick in the balls. Would one day earlier have frickin' killed him?

"What was he having?" I said, trying to sound like I thought it was funny now.

"I don't know," said Trever. He let out a little laugh. "None of that stuff's good for you, though."

I exhaled and shook my head. I felt a lot of things and one of them was incredibly, record-settingly stupid. We didn't need the assistant principal to tell us we were wrong, but it really drove the point home when he did. I looked at Mixer and Bones. Their faces were crash sites of different expressions — relieved, hurt, embarrassed — the gears grinding away in their heads.

"Well, that's good then," Bones managed.

"Yeah, some pretty easy police work. Some troopers were waiting in the drive-thru and they saw him walking across the parking lot. He told them he was on his way home anyway."

"Man," said Mixer.

"Well," I said. "Where was he?"

"Not sure," said Trever. "But apparently they had a hard time recognizing him from his photo. Seems he's made some changes."

"What kind of changes?" I said.

"Sorry," said Trever, "that's all I know. Anyway, you three can go back to class now. I'll let Archie know I caught up with you."

We were in more of a mood to stay and talk about all this, and he must've been used to that, too, because he stood there until I started up the stairs and Mixer and Bones headed back toward shop.

"That's a relief, huh?" said Chaney when I walked back into Spanish. Whoever called must've told her about Tommy turning up. She said it without any Spanish at all, not teacher to student, just person to person, and I guess that surprised me.

"Yeah," I said, returning to my seat.

The blackboard was full of new sentences. I sat there picking out the words I knew and basically just trying to piece my nerves back together. I felt like they'd gone to hang me and the rope broke. Now I was just waiting to be strung up again. But the last few minutes of class just rolled slowly by. The next thing that rang wasn't the phone, it was the bell. I gathered up my stuff and headed to English.

Tommy was alive, I thought, walking alone through the busy hallway. Was Haberman?

"Mr. Haberman is incommunicado this morning," said Ms. Yanoff, once we were all seated. "So once again, the powers that be have seen fit to provide me with a day's wages."

English teachers, where did they get them?

22

Lunch was a hot ham-and-cheese grinder, and it was still sitting in my stomach like a bowling ball when things started happening. We had math in the afternoon on Mondays. The numbers were still the same, but Dantley was usually in a little better mood by then. He was sitting on the front corner of his desk, flipping through his book and trying to find something, when someone knocked on the door. He must've found what he was looking for, because he laid the book down spread-eagle on his desk before walking over.

I didn't look at Mixer or Bones and did my best not to freak out too much. I couldn't keep revving my engine for false alarms, and if it was the real thing, well, there wasn't much I could do about it. I thought maybe I'd try to look innocent, walk out of the room wearing a halo. Or maybe I'd try surprised on for size, like, I wonder what this could be about?

Dantley opened the door a crack and exchanged a few words with someone in the hallway. I couldn't make out what they were saying, and instead of someone coming into the room, Dantley stepped out into the hallway and closed the door behind him. Everyone started talking, and I looked over at Mixer. He just turned and shrugged. He didn't know what was going on and was too worn down to speculate. I looked over at Bones. His eyes were fixed on the front of the room like he expected the next thing to come through the door to be a tear-gas canister.

Instead, it was Dantley. He was two shades whiter and pretty obviously shaken up about something. He didn't say what and just gave us some problems to work out for the rest of the class. I knew he wasn't going to get around to calling on us for the answers, so I didn't bother. He didn't say what he was upset about, but it wasn't hard to figure out.

Sure enough, once we were out in the hallway, Mixer said, "Look out the window."

I looked in the direction he'd nodded and saw a State Police cruiser parked out front. By the time I got to my locker and back, a second one had shown up.

"They know," I said to Mixer. We hadn't waited for Bones.

"About him," he said. "Not about us."

Mixer was right about that, because heading toward the

locker room to change for gym, a Statie walked right by us. We played it pretty cool, I think. Maybe we slowed up some, but we didn't turn around or wet ourselves or anything. It didn't matter anyway. He wasn't looking at us. He passed by on my left, so I got a good look at his gun. Not a revolver like Throckmorton's, some kind of an automatic, all black. The Statie was tall with buzz-cut hair and a little bit of a forward lean to his walk. He was heading toward the office.

"That's it, man," I said, pulling on my shorts.

"We don't know that," said Mixer, closing his locker.

"Come on," I said. We had to communicate in the fewest, most general words possible, but what I was saying was that Haberman was dead.

Mixer wasn't willing to admit that just yet. He spun the dial on his combination lock and said, "I'll see you up there."

"Yeah," I said. I really wasn't in the mood for volleyball.

I passed by Mixer during a game, when he was rotating to the front row and I was rotating back to serve. "We just stood there," I said.

"Shut up," he said, and then he was past me. Someone threw the ball to me, but I wasn't ready for it and it bounced off my chest.

When we were changing afterward, Reedy whipped around the corner. His mouth was already hanging open, so you could see he had news.

"Did you hear?" he said.

It's never cool to come up on someone fast when they're changing, but he had my attention. "What?"

"Haberman's in a coma!"

For a split second, I thought I might join him.

"I said: Haberman's in —"

"I heard you! Christ!" I said.

"Man," said Mixer. "How'd it happen?"

"No one knows!" said Reedy, already turning to tell the next row.

I thought back to the way that tall Statie was walking, like he was chasing off something only he could see, and I knew that wasn't true.

The buses could not come fast enough after that. A coma, I wasn't sure what that'd mean for us, and I couldn't work out the angles with all these cops and kids and distractions around. The only thing I knew for sure was that they didn't know it was us yet. Bones found me at my locker.

"Coma," he said. "It's on the radio and everything."

"And?" I said, letting my voice be overpowered by the end-of-day noise.

"They aren't saying why yet, just that 'an investigation is ongoing.'"

The thoughts that kept me awake the night before hit me again, so close together it might as well've been all at once: tire tracks, boot prints, my fishing gear. Bones still hadn't returned it.

"Great," I said.

"Really?" said Bones.

"No, you idiot."

He shot me a look and headed toward the North Cambria bus.

"Call ya later," he said, but I didn't reply.

I met up with Mixer at his locker.

"What did Captain Ass-hat have to say?" he said.

"Says it's on the radio: 'An investigation is ongoing.'"

"Great."

We headed out to the first Soudley bus. There was a Statie, older than the one from the hallway, on the steps to the main entrance. He was standing next to Throckmarten and watching the buses load. They were talking, their chins sort of shading toward each other but their eyes on the rows of kids climbing into the different buses. I pointed out the trooper to Mixer, even though I was pretty sure he'd seen him already.

"Are you nuts?" Mixer hissed.

"What?" I said. "They'd only expect us to look away if we were guilty."

We sat in the back of the bus and talked about how we were going to kick Tommy's ass when we saw him. My stop came first.

"Check you later," I said, meaning I'd call.

I climbed off the bus and stood there as the door closed behind me and the bus lurched back into gear. I'm not sure

I'd ever been happier to see my little yellow house. I was walking across the lawn and trying to remember what snacks we had left when Tommy came around the far wall. It was like Trever'd said, I almost didn't recognize him at first. His shaggy mop of brown hair was gone, replaced by a short, styled cut. The color was different, too, the brown shading toward blond in places. He had an earring in one ear, and that was new, too.

"Hey," he said.

"Geez, man, look at you."

"Yeah, had an argument with a barber," he said. I looked at his hair. That hadn't happened at some eight-dollar barbershop. "Listen, man. I know you've got questions."

"You got no idea," I said. There were a few things I could've added, just to bust on him. I'd said the same things plenty of times before, but I held up now. There was something in his voice — apology, yeah, but something else, too.

"Can I come in?" he said.

And it's funny he'd put it that way, because what he was really doing was coming out. That thing in his voice, it was hesitation. This was hard for him to say, but he didn't really need to say it to me. I got it now.

It's not like, as a guy, you couldn't get a fancy haircut. It's not like you couldn't get an ear pierced. It's not even like you couldn't drop out of sight for a while. But you sort of step back and take it all together: It's not like you couldn't, but guys like us, we just didn't. I looked at him standing there, with his highlights and his plain steel stud, and I just wanted to punch him in the face, hard. Did he have any idea what we'd done on his account? And now it was like he wasn't even him.

I clenched up my fists, but he just stood his ground. I waited for the anger to lead me somewhere, but it didn't. I knew if I wanted to clock him once, he'd let me, and I guess that's how I knew this was the same tough bastard I'd known the week before.

"Sure," I said. "But don't try anything."

He let out a small laugh, not much more than a puff of breath.

"You picked a good week to be gone," I said, opening the door. I couldn't find it in me to hate him.

23

I didn't tell him what we'd done while he was off "finding himself" or whatever. I figured it was better for all of us if he didn't know. That way, he couldn't be charged with anything, and there'd be one less person to testify against us. Of course, if anyone could keep a secret, it was pretty clear it was Tommy.

"What about that whole Natalie thing?" I was saying. "All that 'she's so hot' and stuff? Was that just bull?"

"I don't know, man," he said. We were sitting at opposite ends of the dining room table. I think I sort of wanted to have some furniture between us. "I was probably hoping more than pretending at first, but basically, yeah, I picked the hottest chick in class and went around telling everyone I had it bad for her. It seemed like the right thing to say, and it didn't seem like I'd ever have to put my money where my mouth was."

"You'd be surprised the mouths that end up on Natalie these days," I said, but I didn't explain that one, either. "Man, you had me fooled. You seemed so nervous around her."

"Yeah, well, I guess bad acting looks a lot like real nerves," he said. "But that's what it got to be for me, man: acting, pretending. I was pretending every day of my life, first to myself and then to you guys. That's what I can't do anymore. I've got to . . ."

And I knew from the buildup that he was going to uncork some feel-good expression, like "be true to me" or some crap like that. He just let his voice trail off, because he must've remembered that I wasn't the right audience for that kind of thing. This wasn't *Oprah*.

"Well, you know," he said after a bit.

"Yeah, I know," I said, and there was a little more silence. "But why Dantley's class? Why'd you lose it in there?"

"'Cause he knew. He'd been hounding me big-time, 'cause he knew exactly what I was."

"I didn't even know," I said. "How the hell would Dantley?"

"Seriously?" said Tommy.

"Seriously."

"Because Dantley's queer as hell."

"No frickin' way!"

"Yeah, totally."

And I just had to shake my head. It was like, all these years of calling people homos and fags, and I couldn't tell the real thing when it was two feet in front of me. Man, I thought, these small-town queers, the CIA ought to sign 'em up.

And I had other questions. "Manchester again?" I said.

"Nah."

"Same guy though."

"Yeah."

"Is he one, too?"

"Yeah."

He didn't offer details, and I didn't push for them. There's only so accepting a guy can be expected to be in a day, you know?

"Listen, whatever you're thinking, he helped me a lot. He . . ."

I cut him off: "What about the guys?"

"Let me tell Mixer," he said.

"You might want to skip Bones for now," I said. I wondered if he was dumb enough to still have that club.

"I was planning on it."

"How'd you get here anyway?"

"Biked it."

"Oh, man, enjoy the climb," I said, because Soudley was down the valley from North Cambria.

"Good for me," he said. "Builds character."

"Just be careful it doesn't mess up your hair."

He flipped me off and let himself out, and I just sat there at the table for a long time. Man, I thought. Tommy was going to have problems in school. Serious problems, and things were going to change between him and us. A week ago, I would've felt sorry for him, but right now, I had my own problems.

I went to the kitchen for a slice of cheese. Tommy was walking his bike across the lawn toward the road. He got on, heading toward Mixer's house. He was leaving, and I'd completely forgotten to kick his ass. I wondered if Mixer would.

24

It took them two days total to come for us. I'm surprised it took them that long. I figured that Haberman'd finally come to, but that wasn't the case. Bones'd picked up a little knickknack when he'd gone into the kitchen to clean himself off, and he'd forgotten to wipe it down. It was a wedge of amber with a real wasp set inside. It was sitting on the windowsill above the sink, and I guess Bones wanted a closer look. I'd be madder about that, but they pulled a partial of mine off the door frame, from where Haberman tried to shut it on me. All of our prints were on file from "Missing Children: Don't Be a Victim" Day back at Soudley Central. I think Mixer was just a case of guilt by association, at least until they found his boots.

They picked Bones up at the bus stop. He got a State Police cruiser all to himself. It was like he was waiting there for them to arrest him. He said he didn't even see them until the cruiser pulled right up in front of him, and that's sort of the way it was waiting for the bus. The cars just bled by out of focus.

It was Throckmorton who collected Mixer and me. Not at our stops but just after. He pulled the bus over. He lit it up with the flashers and pulled it right over. Mixer and I were talking about Tommy, of course, wondering if he'd be at school and kind of deciding how we'd handle it if he was. I heard the chatter pick up around us before I saw the pale blue light reflected on the ceiling. Then I felt the bus slow down and pull off to the side.

Mixer was turned around already so I just asked him, "Who?"

"Sheriff," he said.

That seemed better than a Statie to me, I guess because I'd met Throckmorton before. The devil you know, right? What had he said to me then, "I'll see you around"? I wondered if, after all those years on the job, he could see a kid and just tell.

The bus driver opened the door and Throckmorton and his deputy climbed on. It was always weird to see adults climbing onto school buses, like how the teachers were always last aboard for field trips. It was even weirder when they were wearing guns. For a second, I thought of hiding, ducking down, and maybe crawling between seats. I knew our schoolmates would give us up, though, not all of them but probably most. They'd rat us out and then wait around to have a gold star stuck to their foreheads.

The bus got quiet when Throckmorton's eyes started scanning the seats. When he called out our names, it boomed inside the hollow space, Grand Canyon–style. It was probably the first time anyone had said Mixer's real name that year. We put on some I-can't-believe-this body language, but basically we just stood up and walked down the aisle. There wasn't much else to do.

"Come on, boys," Throckmorton said, extending his hand. Then he sort of cut ahead of the other guy so that he wouldn't have to walk down the stairs with his back directly to us. That was what deputies were for, I figured.

We kept quiet in the back of the police car. There was a layer of that special glass or plastic or whatever it was between the front and back seats. I wasn't sure if they'd be able to hear us if we kept it low, but they might've had some kind of device or something, maybe a recorder, and I didn't feel much like talking anyway.

I just watched the town go by. How many times had I been driven down this same road, and why did it look different now? It was still early, but I'm sure a few people saw me back there when we blew through downtown. If even one person had, it'd be all over town by noon. My mom must've known already. They were probably already in my room, collecting my boots and stuff.

The flashers weren't on anymore, but we were doing seventy, easy. They'd turned the lights off as soon as we were in the backseat. It seemed a little backward to me, but I guess they were in more of a hurry to grab us than to get us any-where. We pulled out and passed the bus, which was still parked on the side of the road, with the tires on one side cutting tracks into someone's lawn. Dozens of eyes looked down as we went by, with exactly half as many mouths flapping. They'd be talking about this at the Tits for years.

We rocketed by the sheriff's office, so I knew we were headed for the State Police barracks over in Canterbridge. I sort of wondered how that worked, jurisdiction-wise. Bones was already there when they brought us down to the holding cells. There were four cells total, and we were the only guests. They allowed us each one phone call, just like on TV. I figured my mom already knew, so I asked if there was any way I could check my e-mail instead. There wasn't, so I called my mom anyway. Four words for you: Not a good call. They put us each in our own cell, and the tall trooper I'd seen at the school stood straight across from us, arms folded. We could talk if we wanted, and he could listen.

"Do you guys know what this is about?" said Bones. He was talking to us, but it was for the trooper's benefit.

"Give it a rest," I said. What was the guy going to do, run out and tell them we were innocent? And Bones was a bad actor anyway.

I think he was doing something else there, too, trying to get us all together on something, even if it was just bad acting. He wanted us all together, because I think he knew this little group was about to come apart.

And he was right. The door at the far end opened and another trooper walked in. He stopped just a few steps in, just close enough to be heard.

"All right, Benton," he said, guessing wrong and looking at Mixer. "You're up first."

25

They tried Bones as an adult. It seemed like they'd been doing that to a lot of teens lately, but I guess that's because the only cases you hear about are the real bad ones. But Bones was sixteen, almost seventeen, and he'd done the damage, so they tried him as an adult for attempted murder. Some people said it should've been assault instead, but I can't say I disagreed with the charge.

In fact, I'll never be able to say I disagreed, because I testified against him. I'm on the record. I don't know if you've ever seen one of those nature shows on crocodiles, but they do this thing called a death roll. They grab hold of an animal with their teeth and just start spinning. They tear it all to hell. That's pretty much how I rolled on Bones. It sort of seemed like piling on at the end, but I guess that's the way people get put away.

Mixer and me had the same lawyer. Mixer's folks paid for most of him, but my mom chipped in. The guy was real slick. He wanted Mixer to talk, too, but Mixer wouldn't testify against anyone. He refused to answer almost everything on the grounds that almost everything was "liable to incriminate" him. It's called taking the fifth, or pleading the fifth maybe, I forget. Either way, Mixer spent most of a morning doing it.

I could've done that, too. I mean, I'd never seen myself as the kind of guy who'd squeal. Yeah, Bones was out of control, but it was still Bones. I'd grown up with him. And there wasn't really anything in it for me. I was a juvenile. I hadn't swung the club, and no one was saying I had. There was a maximum they were going to be able to do to me, and that was already running up against the minimum people around here were going to accept.

But I went ahead and testified anyway. I put it all down on paper for Throckmorton, and when he asked me if I wanted someone to read it off for me, I said, "Nah, I'll do it." And I took the stand and read it all out, while the lady sat there and typed it all on to skinny paper with that little machine.

If you've never been in a courtroom, then it's not what you're thinking. Or it's half what you're thinking, but the other half is like Bingo night at the VFW. It's a little cut-rate. The chairs for the audience aren't folding chairs, but they're just one step up from that. They're made out of the same hollow metal and have vinyl pads for your back and butt. The floors are just floors, like at school. The jury box and the judge's desk are made out of wood, but it's just regular wood, like from a kitchen set.

I wasn't expecting marble thrones or anything, but it all looks heftier and nicer on TV. And the judge is pretty much always some really distinguished-looking guy on TV, but he was just this normal little dude. I would've pegged him for a dentist if it wasn't for the robe, but even that looked at least half polyester.

Anyway, the dentist was sitting above me and to the right when they swore me in. He seemed kind of bored, to be honest. Bones was sitting at a table out in front. He was staring daggers at me, because you can't stare clubs. Mixer was looking down at the floor. Tommy was in the back, and he looked like he couldn't believe any of this. My mom had her chin up, and she almost looked proud. I was thinking, Don't be, Mom. It's not like I'm up here collecting an award.

The jury was just this random group of adults off to my left. It was like they'd gone into a Dunkin' Donuts at three P.M. and rounded up everyone there. It was sort of a stacked deck, too, because it's supposed to be "a jury of your peers," right, but the youngest one there was at least twice our age. They were looking at me like I was an exhibit at the zoo, like the North American ring-tailed delinquent or something. They were getting a good look at my eye, because they were on that side.

Everyone else in the room was looking at me, too. I cleared my throat and got to it. My voice was shaking a little at first, and I sort of hated myself for that. I really didn't want to be up there.

You know why I was, why I testified? I'll tell you. It was the way Haberman used to call us gentlemen. "Right this way, gentlemen." It was the way he called me Mr. Benton. I used to think he was making fun of me — I mean, I wasn't exactly walking around school in a tuxedo — but then, I used to think that pretty much everyone was making fun of me, looking at me, whatever. I was pretty quick on the draw when it came to taking offense. All that stuff seems kind of small now, after seeing a man beaten like that in his own living room.

I guess I just realized that Haberman actually meant it. He was showing me some respect, and I just wasn't used to seeing any. He wasn't picking on me in class, he was giving me a chance. I think maybe I knew it as soon as he opened the door for me. And how did I repay him for that? I sat there and watched him bleed on his own floor.

So now I was repaying him this way, because I realized one other thing, too, at just about the same time: Bones was a damn psycho. Haberman's house, the house in the woods . . . dude should pretty much be kept on a leash outside. Because friendships ended. Damn right they did, and for a lot less than all this. I appreciated him sticking up for me in like sixth grade, but at some point you've got to move on. It just stops being cool to lash out, to hurt people who haven't hurt you. And it stops being OK to just let that happen.

So yeah, I testified. Bones was like, You'll be sorry, man. And I was like, Yeah, maybe I will, but not for seven to ten years, bitch.

26

Mixer and me got juvie. I finally realized what Mixer was saying that night when I got out of the truck: "We are fifteen." They sent us to different places, but I can't imagine his sucks any more than mine does. Juvenile detention is like a school you can't leave. And it's even worse than that, if you can believe it, because everyone in there has some kind of major damage, and they all think they've got to be cold-blooded 24/7. I don't have it too bad that way. They think I killed a teacher, and I'm not going to tell them I didn't.

Anyway, that's my deal. I'll be here for the next few years, and I figure I'll have to move away from Soudley once I get out, in order to find any kind of a job and start saving up to buy that truck, the one with the plow on the front.

In the meantime, I've got a lot of time to kill. I finished that book, for one. That dude, Raskolnikov, he didn't get away with it, either. That didn't surprise me one bit. The dumbass gave himself up, confessed. They shipped him off to Siberia, which turns out to be a real place. I always thought it was just a figure of speech, sent to Siberia, like Podunk or Palookaville.

There was this one really cool line: "his dream seemed strangely to persist." Sort of trippy, right? And thinking about what had happened, about Bones swinging away and me just standing there frozen and the red of the blood and all that . . . It really did seem like a dream now. As for persisting, that was a freaking understatement.

Anyway, once I finished the book, I wrote Haberman about it. I guess that was my way of saying sorry. I'm not going to write out the whole letter here, because it was between me and him. I mostly talked about his class. "I think I get what you were saying with the barrel and the words on the board and all that," I wrote. "Like at the end of the book" — I threw that in so he'd know I finished — "the dude confessed, but even at the trial, he sort of had to convince them that he'd done it. And, I mean, they sent him away, but is it really 'punishment' if that's what he wanted?"

Stuff like that. I know he got it, because you know what he did? That old dude sent me a carton of Camels, a full frickin' carton. Do you know what a big deal that is in here?

That many Humpies in one place is like the damn promised land, but Haberman wasn't going to use them. One thing about spending all that time in a coma is that it cleared all the nicotine right out of his system. He went cold turkey out cold, kicked it clean.

I opened that package and it was like Christmas morning. I read his little note:

I'm glad you liked the book. You are more gifted than you know, and this is still the first chapter for you. I wish you the best. As for the cigarettes, I won't be needing them.

I folded up the note and put it in my lockbox with the smokes. Won't be needing them? His loss, I figured.